SANTA ANA PUBLIC LIBRARY
NEWHOPE BRANCH
D0429017

The Universe of Fair

The Universe of
FAIR
Leslie Bulion
drawings by Frank W. Dormer
PEACHTREE
ATLANTA

Published by
PEACHTREE PUBLISHERS
1700 Chattahoochee Avenue
Atlanta, Georgia 30318-2112
www.peachtree-online.com

Book design and composition by Melanie McMahon Ives

Manufactured in 2012 by Lake Book Manufacturing, Inc. in Melrose Park, Illinois, in the United States of America
10 9 8 7 6 5 4 3 2 1
First Edition

Library of Congress Cataloging-in-Publication Data

Bulion, Leslie, 1958-
The universe of fair / written by Leslie Bulion.
p. cm.
Summary: Eleven-year-old Miller Sanford has tried to prove himself mature enough to be on his own at the annual fair, but instead he is handed responsibility for his six-year-old sister and her friends, leading to a series of mysteries and mishaps.
ISBN 978-1-56145-634-5 / 1-56145-634-9
[1. Agricultural exhibitions--Fiction. 2. Responsibility--Fiction. 3. Babysitters--Fiction. 4. Brothers and sisters--Fiction. 5. Family life--Connecticut--Fiction. 6. Connecticut--Fiction.] I. Title.
PZ7.B911155Uni 2012
[Fic]--dc23

2011020974

For Carrie

—L. B.

1
THE FORCE FIELD

On the way home from school on the bus I'm staring off into space and thinking about how weird it is that I ended up to be me, Miller Sanford, from Holmsbury, Connecticut. I think how much more likely it is that I would have been born in China, because there are more than a billion people there and only three hundred million here, and even less in Connecticut, and way less in Holmsbury.

Then I think that if I was born in China, I'd probably be allowed to ride my bicycle home from middle school. Unless I had the same mom in China that I have now. Which I guess I'd want, even if she wouldn't let me ride my bicycle home from school. Which she wouldn't.

What's even weirder to think about is that if my molecules and atoms and electrons and quarks were put together in a different way, I could just as easily be an earthworm.

Or a rock. Maybe I *am* a rock. Maybe I'm a rock that just thinks I'm an eleven-and-a-half-year-old boy.

"How do you know you're not really a rock?" I ask my friend Lewis, who's in the seat behind me.

"Because rocks don't make movies," Lewis says. He waves his hand sideways, keeping his eyes glued to the flip screen of his video camera. "Stand up and look out the window."

Lewis makes movies every minute he's not in school—and some of the minutes he is, if the teacher steps out and Lewis has time to get his camera from her desk drawer. It's a hand-me-down video camera from his uncle, which is why his parents let him take it everywhere. He has some really big movie ideas, some funny ideas, and some ideas I just don't get. I'm in all of his movies, but I don't have to act. I'm just me, Miller.

I look out the bus window as we pass through town and right away my heart starts thumping and I grin like crazy, because where poles and canvas lay in heaps on the grass this morning, huge white tents now billow in the breeze and they fill the entire town green.

"It's ready!" I shout.

A police officer in the middle of the street holds up her hand and the bus stops short in front of the library. I have to grab the edge of the open bus window so I don't fall over.

"That was a good shot," Lewis says, peering at his screen.

"Sit down!" the bus driver yells. "All of you just SIT DOWN! You'll get to see the Fair when it opens tomorrow, same as every year."

The bus lurches forward again, so I face sideways, then backward in my seat and I can't stop looking until we go around the bend and pull away from the Fair's force field. I don't know why the bus driver didn't feel it, but she didn't, because if she had, she never would have said "same as every year."

The Holmsbury Fair is not just a rerun of the same rides and the same games, and the foods and the crafts and the animals. And the high school jazz band, the frog races, the day off from school, and wondering whether you got a first or second or third place for your giant zucchini are not the "same as every year" either. Every year at the Fair you're one whole year older, so nothing is the same at all.

Every year, it's like the force field pulls you through a "next year" fold in space-time because the Fair feels different and you feel different, and the change happens all at once on Fair Friday, not little by little so you never notice it like all the rest of the growing you do.

The bus stops and goes, stops and goes along Main Street, where the houses are crooked and old but mostly not in a haunted house kind of way. They're built right up to the road like they were three hundred years ago. I wonder if the new houses near the edges of Holmsbury are set way back from the street so no one can see what people are watching on their big-screen TVs. Maybe people in colonial times were a lot nosier and they wanted to see into their neighbors' houses from the road even if there weren't big-screen TVs.

We turn off Main Street and rumble along a few more streets that are more like mine, with houses that aren't as old as the crooked ones, but are still close enough together for you to talk to your neighbors from the front porches. Which my mom likes. And my dad doesn't.

My dad is an electrician, but he always takes this whole Fair week off from his regular work and comes and goes at odd hours. When he's at the fairgrounds, he helps hook up electricity for the fundraiser booths. Whenever he's home, he bakes. Every day he bakes a different pie so he can decide which kind is the best to enter in the adult baking competition at the Fair. We kids get to be the taste-testers on all of the practice ones. Lewis always comes over a lot, but he comes over even more during Fair week because of the pies.

When we're getting off at my corner, Lewis turns on the steps and aims his camera back at the bus driver. "Are you going to the Fair?" he asks her. He presses the Record button with his thumb.

"Put that camera away and walk down facing frontwards," the driver tells him. *"Are you going to the Fair?"* She repeats Lewis's question. "Do these kids think the parking lot shuttle bus drives itself?" she mutters as if we're not there anymore.

"And...cut," Lewis says.

The driver closes the door and the bus rumbles away.

We walk along my street and I don't talk to Lewis because I can see that he's thinking about his movie. He's told me that this is going to be a Holmsbury Fair movie, but he doesn't have the story all worked out yet. Sometimes he just shoots a bunch of scenes and makes a story out of what he gets. He's really good at that.

After a minute he says, "Maybe I should go to Elmsville in the morning and get a shot of the sad kids who have to go to school tomorrow when we don't."

"Fair Friday is the single best day of the whole year in Holmsbury and tomorrow is going to be our best one ever, and you want to go to *Elmsville?*" I take out my key and stick it in our kitchen door lock.

"Right. Never mind." Lewis raises his camera. "Okay. Go." He aims at my hand and then at the widening space next to the kitchen door as I push it open.

I don't know why Lewis does this because he already has about six hundred and seventy-three shots of Cooper the Wonderdog bounding closer and closer to the camera until his yellow face looks pulled back around the edges and stretched in the middle, so his nose turns into a big, fat, black hockey puck. Cooper always gets dog snot on the lens, which Lewis thinks is funny. Every time.

"Good boy, Coop," Lewis says. He wipes the lens. "You are very camera friendly."

The truth is our big, goofy Labrador doesn't embarrass easily, which is more than you can say for a lot of people Lewis videos.

I let Cooper out into the backyard. Lewis follows him with the camera.

"Beee-yoo-ti-ful," I hear him tell Coop.

Like I said, the Wonderdog is not easily embarrassed.

What is embarrassing is that I am eleven and a half and in sixth grade, and today is the first day in my entire life that my mom is letting me come home from school without her being here. Since my dad's working at the fairgrounds and my mom found out just before she left for work that she has to stay late for a meeting, I'm finally being allowed to stay home on my own. For thirty-five whole minutes.

Lately I've been trying to show how responsible and careful I am, so being home alone is a great opportunity. Although Cooper is here and Lewis is here, too, so technically I'm not even alone. Lewis is an expert at being left alone because he has two older brothers who are supposed to watch him and don't—which his mom and dad sort of know but also sort of don't do anything about because, as Lewis explains, he's the third boy and they're tired.

I empty Coop's water bowl and refill it with clean water from the kitchen tap. That is me being responsible. I close the front door and lock it from the inside. That is me being responsible *and* careful, even though I could walk right into almost every house on my street right now and jump on all the beds because no one around here locks their doors, and even my parents don't when they're home. I realize that the jumping on the beds part would not be considered responsible. Or careful.

"You could take out the garbage." Lewis comes in from the backyard with Cooper. "That shows you're responsible."

"Maybe," I say. "Or does taking out the garbage show I'm not careful, because someone could see me doing it and assume that I'm home alone?"

"Your mother is nice, Mill, but trying to think like she thinks gives me a headache," Lewis says.

"I *have* to think like her. I have to do everything right or she'll never let me be on my own at the Fair tomorrow."

"Maybe you can be so responsible and careful she'll let you come on Saturday, too," Lewis says hopefully.

"Forget Saturday," I say. "You know none of us ever goes on a Saturday. My mom says it's 'unmanageably crowded' and if anyone wanted to meet up with her there she'd never hear her phone ring and—" I snap my fingers. "I forgot to check our voice mail."

The little green light is blinking, so I push the button.

Beep!

"Hello, Milly?"

Eleven-and-a-half-year-old boys named Miller are *not* called "Milly." My mom is a very smart person with a graduate degree in social work, but this is something she can't seem to learn.

"My meeting is running late, so I'll have to ask you to meet Penelope at the elementary bus at four twenty-five."

I groan. The message keeps going.

"The bus driver will beep if you're not there since she doesn't let first-graders off alone, even though I'm always there and she's never had to beep before. If no one's there to walk Penny home, she'll have to drive her along the rest of the route and back to school, so why don't you go out at four-twenty, just to be safe?"

My mom talks faster.

"Check your watch with the kitchen clock to be sure you have the right time. Andrew's mom is home. You and Penny are welcome to stay with her until I get there."

I groan again. Her voice speeds up even more.

"Dad left a pie where he always does, up on top of the refrigerator—"

BEEP!

The rest of the message is cut off, which always happens because my mom's instructions include many details. She tells my dad our voice mail should have more message time, but he smiles and says we all have our limits.

Lewis picks up his camera and aims it at the top of the refrigerator. "Should we do pie before your sister's bus gets here?" he asks.

"I guess so." I trudge across the kitchen. "I can't believe I have to end my first time home alone by going over to a six-year-old's house."

"Yeah, but getting Penny off the bus shows you're responsible."

I stop in mid-trudge. "Wait!" I say. "I can be even *more* responsible than that. My mom said we are *welcome* to stay at Andrew's—she didn't say we *have* to. I'll get my sister off of the bus, then I'll bring her home and watch her myself!"

"*Dun-dun-dun-duhhhhnn!*" Lewis imitates scary movie music.

"Come on. How hard could it be?" I wave away his warning. "This is my chance to prove once and for all how responsible and careful I am. Then I won't have to be the only Holmsbury sixth-grader in the entire history of the Fair who has to stay with his parents on Fair Friday!"

"Well," Lewis says, "the Fair does start tomorrow. This might be your best shot."

"I'm going to do everything right," I tell him. "Until my mom gets home, I'll be so nice to Painy it'll be revolting!"

Lewis raises his eyebrows in my general direction.

"Okay, *Penny*. I'll be nice to *Penny*. I'll even be nice to Andrew or Lou-Ann, if they come over to play with her." Now that I've said that, I'm hoping it won't be Andrew because being nice probably includes staying in the same room with him for more than three minutes. Which I usually don't, since he's a complete hazard.

"I need to fortify myself," I say. "Let's test pie."

I stand on tiptoe and reach way back to slide today's practice pie from the top of the fridge. I have to be careful because it's a mile-high lemon meringue baked in our big blue pie dish. I turn around with the heavy dish balanced in my hands and almost hit the camera as Lewis zooms in for a close-up. "Whoa," I say. The topping shivers.

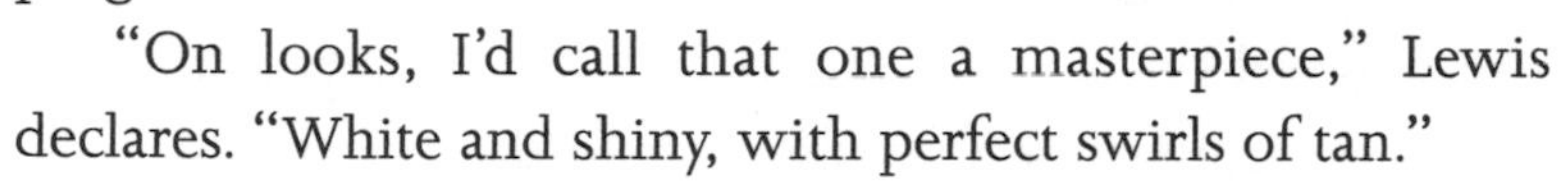

"On looks, I'd call that one a masterpiece," Lewis declares. "White and shiny, with perfect swirls of tan."

When I slice through the meringue topping with the pie cutter, it stays in a firm but airy mound. Way to go, Dad, I think. I cut two huge wedges, leaving a big empty space in the pie dish.

"And...cut," Lewis says. He pours us milks.

I deliver each forkful to my mouth with my eyes closed because I don't want to mix any other senses in with the tasting. I am hugely happy that these molecules and atoms and electrons and quarks lined up to be this particular lemon meringue pie.

"This one is the winner," Lewis says reverently. "Your dad is the king of pie."

"You said that after you tasted the triple-berry pie, the apple crumb pie, and the chocolate pecan pie."

"I know."

"And you said it after the sour cherry pie and the pumpkin cream pie, too," I remind him.

"All true," he says. "But this time I mean it even more."

"Ung gno," I say, which is "I know" with my mouth full. Lewis is right. This pie is absolutely the best.

I hear a rumbling sound coming from up the street. The kitchen clock says four twenty-five.

"The bus!"

I launch myself away from the table and scrabble at the kitchen door lock, then blast outside. Cooper dives through my legs and I trip down our front steps on top of him. As I'm untangling myself, four kids fan down the steps of the bus in a mathematically impossible number of directions. None of them is my sister. The driver leans on the horn. I brush my hands on my pants and sprint up the street. Things are still basically under control. As I run by, Andrew's mother waves from her front door.

"I'm all set!" I shout to her. "We'll be at home."

When I get to the bus, Penelope whips a flat purple and green cardboard ring out of the open door so it hits me square between the eyes.

"We made Frisbees in art," she says, marching down the steps. "Mine flies perfectly straight." She looks behind me at Lewis. "Did you get that on the movie? Want me to do it again?"

"No, he doesn't," I say.

Cooper, who is not supposed to be out on the street without a leash, picks that moment to chase a squirrel under the bus.

"Get your dog, kid," the driver says.

"C'mon, Coop, c'mon boy," I coax. I can see his yellow tail but he's sensitive about it so I don't pull him out that way. So far, things are not going quite as smoothly as I'd hoped.

"Hey, Coop," Lewis calls. He leans down and points his camera under the bus.

When Cooper turns around to lick the camera, I grab him by the collar and haul him out.

"Where's Mom?" Penny asks. She's standing on the sidewalk, too close to the open bus door. The driver wants to get going and my sister is sort of in the way, so I nudge her away from the bus.

"Mom's at a meeting," I say. "She's going to be late, so she left me in charge." I present this information in a no-big-deal kind of voice.

"You can't be in charge," Penny says in her louder-than-necessary six-year-old voice. "You're not allowed to be in charge because you're not old enough. You're not very much older than me."

"YES I AM," I say in an even louder, getting-exasperated voice. "Right now I'm almost twice as old as you."

Lewis, who is trying to look out for my best interest, gives me a shove.

I take a deep breath. "I mean," I say, starting again, "Mom called and asked me to get you at the bus because she is going to be a little late."

"You are late," Penny tells me.

"Dad left us pie," I say, changing the subject.

"What kind?"

"Lemon meringue."

"I love lemon meringue pie." Andrew appears out of nowhere, giving me a heart attack as usual. He's home-schooled, so he doesn't keep regular hours.

"Want to come over?" Penny asks Andrew.

"Yes." He bobs his head up and down.

Penny looks at me. "Well?"

"Well what?"

"Mom always holds my hand on the way back from the bus." She sticks her Frisbee flinger out and waits.

Holmsbury Fair Friday has always been the best day of the year. If I prove to my parents I'm responsible enough to be on my own, tomorrow will be the best day of my entire life. But if I'm the only sixth-grader in town who still has to stay with his parents, tomorrow will be the worst Fair Friday ever. So I take Penny's hand and Lewis takes Cooper's collar and Andrew continues to move in his little parallel universe and we walk home.

I cut pieces of pie for Penny and Andrew and Lewis pours them milks. I have to give a clean fork to Andrew after he drops his on the floor. Then the other member of the six-year-old Pest Pack shows up, so I give Lou-Ann her piece of pie, and Andrew slips his plate in there and mixes me up, so he gets seconds.

"That's it," I say when Andrew holds up his plate for the third time. "This last piece is for my mom."

"She's gonna love it," Lewis says. His camera lingers on the last slice of pie.

I make a big tent of foil over the whole pie dish so my mom will get the full effect of the mile-high meringue and I put it back on top of the refrigerator. I notice Lou-Ann craning her neck to try and see.

"Off limits," I tell her.

She watches everything but never talks, which is a little eerie. The phone rings.

"Phone!" Andrew calls out helpfully.

Mom has told me to let the call go to voice mail and listen first if I'm ever home alone, so I don't answer yet.

"Miller has to listen to the message so he knows who it is," Penelope informs the other first-graders at our kitchen table. "He's not much older than we are."

I grit my teeth and glare at the wall.

"He's just being careful," Lewis explains. "Careful and *responsible.*"

The phone rings again.

"How old are you, exactly?" Andrew wants to know.

I take a deep breath. Or four. "Why don't you all go out in the backyard," I tell them. "Play tag with Coop or something."

Cooper's a great chase dog, so the Pest Pack tumbles out the back door, leaving their dishes and forks all over the table. Lewis films them on the way out, and I clean up while the phone rings a third and a fourth time and finally goes to voice mail. I wait while the caller listens to the outgoing message and I hear silence. Then I hear, "Miller? Miller? It's Mom. Are you there?"

There is a hint of worry in her voice, which is no surprise since my mom has perfected worrying into its own branch of science. I pick up the phone. I'll be happy to reassure her that there is nothing for her to worry about. Nothing at all. I didn't go to Andrew's house, but I have done everything else that needs to be done. I am being super-responsible and trustworthy, too.

"Hi, Mom. Everything's great. I got Pain—um—Penny off the bus, and Lewis is here with me and everyone had a snack and now they're playing in the backyard."

"I called Andrew's mother first," Mom says. "She told me you were at our house. Are you sure you're doing okay with all of the kids over there?"

"Yes, Mom. Everything's fine." I nod at Lewis to show him my plan is working.

I hear other people's voices in the background. Mom says something I don't understand.

"What did you say, Mom?" I ask.

I hear mumbling and realize that she's got her hand over the phone and is talking to someone in her office, not to me. She works with teenagers who need all kinds of help, which keeps her pretty busy. The teenagers give her many ideas for things to worry about, but she's really good at it. Her job, I mean. *And* worrying.

I want to show her she doesn't have to worry about things here. "Mom? I filled Cooper's water bowl and now I'm cleaning up the snack dishes."

"Yes, okay, honey. Please be sure to call Andrew's mom if you need anything. I'm just about to head home. We'll need to make a new plan for tomorrow."

My heart does a flutter flip. I motion frantically to Lewis, hit speakerphone, and hold the receiver out between us.

"Great!" I say. "I have an idea for the plan—"

"Did you get my message about the pie?" Mom interrupts me. Which she usually doesn't.

"Yeah, and I saved—"

"So you saw Dad's note?"

Note? "I didn't—"

"We'll take care of it at the fairgrounds," Mom says. "I'm on my way. Thanks for being so responsible, Miller."

Click.

"Take care of what?" I hang up the phone.

"What note?" Lewis asks.

"I didn't see any note." I look around the kitchen. "Maybe it's up here." I pat around on top of the refrigerator, but I don't feel anything. I pull a chair over and climb up. "There it is." I see a piece of paper with a line of tape dangling from it, and I reach way back behind the blue dish to get it. "It must have fallen off of the pie. Hey, did you hear my mom call me *responsible?*"

I climb down and read my Dad's note out loud to Lewis's camera:

DEAR MILLER,

NO TIME TO COME HOME LATER AND BAKE ANOTHER ONE LIKE I PLANNED, SO THIS PIE'S GOT TO BE THE WINNER! PLEASE PUT FOIL OVER IT AND BRING IT TO THE BAKING BOOTH TONIGHT WHEN YOU GUYS COME OVER. AND GRAB THE ENTRY FORM TOO. THANKS!

LOVE, DAD

The generous slice of pie I ate is now a chunk of lead in my stomach. I drag my eyes over to the side of the refrigerator where my dad's Fair entry form has been all week, stuck on with a magnet. On the line that says "Variety"—the line that has been blank all week—he has written in "Lemon Meringue."

"And...cut." Lewis lowers the camera.

I stare at the foil-covered dish on top of the refrigerator. I gulp. "I'll probably have to stay with my parents at the Fair until I'm a hundred," I tell Lewis.

2
THE THEORY OF EVERYTHING

If you don't count Lou-Ann's bloody nose or Andrew stepping in a Cooperpile and then throwing up under the bushes, the next twenty minutes I'm in charge here go pretty well. From the backyard, I hear my mom's car pull into the driveway. I grab the shovel I just finished using so she'll see I've been responsibly policing the yard. This is a much harder job now that I have to hunt for Cooperpiles under the first yellow, orange, and red fallen leaves.

Lewis hears my mom's car, too. The reason I know he hears it is because he zooms across the patio and through our back kitchen door at the speed of light, and with enough positive momentum to propel him through the kitchen and out the front in a blur my mom will not be able to recall when she finds out about the pie. I'm not surprised at this since Lewis already mentioned that he would not need to include any "pie news" scenes in his Holmsbury

Fair movie. I told him that was okay, because I'd rather do that scene with no audience. I am hoping to deliver the pie news in a way that makes me still seem responsible and careful enough to go to the Fair on my own tomorrow. Timing will be everything.

"Mommy!" my sister shouts.

She runs inside with the other two kids trailing her like she's a magnet. None of them know we weren't supposed to eat the pie so they can't tell on me, even though telling is one of Painy's favorite activities.

Good, I think.

But they all know exactly what they had for snack and how delicious it was.

Bad, I think.

I dash inside and just about choke when I hear my sister saying, "...and Andrew had two pieces but now he has a stomachache and Cooper met the bus driver and Lou-Ann hit me with her nose."

Now that is real talent. My sister can spoil everything without even trying. So much for having the pie scene without an audience. So much for timing.

"Mom," I try to explain, "I didn't mean to..." I don't finish my sentence.

My mom is standing at the kitchen counter staring at a pad of yellow legal paper. She is not facing Penny, or me, or any of us. Her cell phone is next to the pad. She takes a sip of water from a glass and puts it down. Then she writes something on the pad. I'm pretty sure she hasn't heard anything anyone has said.

"Mommy," Penny scolds. "I'm telling you my day and you're not listening."

Mom looks up like she's just realized we're all there. "Okay, kiddos," she says to Lou-Ann and Andrew. "It's almost dinnertime, so you two ought to head for home."

It is safe to assume that she has not put two and two together on the subject of pie mathematics. A little seed of hope sprouts in the bottom of my stomach.

Andrew whines, "I don't think I can eat dinner after all that—"

"Running around," I blurt. "They were really running around out in the yard." I go over and pull out Andrew's chair and help him to his feet. Then I do the same for Lou-Ann. Quickly.

"I hope you saved some of that running-around energy for the Fair tomorrow," Mom says. "It's a big day!"

"Tomorrow is the same size as every other day," Penny points out.

"Well, yes." Mom smiles for a second. Then she presses her lips in a line. "I'm sorry, but I've got to make a call. Miller will watch you two walk home. I'll be right here if anyone needs me."

I sigh. I feel ridiculous watching these kids walk a few houses up the street, something their own parents don't bother to do.

"No one has to watch me," Andrew says. "I'm okay." He pulls on the kitchen doorknob and the door flies open and hits him in the head. He staggers back a step. "I'm perfectly okay," he says.

"*I'd* better watch you," Penny says. "I'm six, and Miller's not much older." She shoots a pointed look in my direction, as if it's my fault Andrew doesn't know how to work a door.

I want us all to get out of here before the idea that I'm not much older than six takes up any of Mom's brain cells.

"Let's go," I tell Lou-Ann and Andrew.

I stand at the end of our driveway while they zing up the street between the trunks of the curbside maples and the telephone poles like pinballs. Walking on the sidewalk must be a seven-year-old skill, I think.

I also think that if you have shown that you are responsible enough to be home alone, to take care of annoying first-graders when your mom is late, and to watch them take a year to travel three and five houses up the street, then you should finally be trusted to go to the Holmsbury Fair with your friends—just like every other sixth-grader in town gets to do on Fair Friday, when everyone's parents are working in the booths and even your teachers are there, and everyone in other towns is still at work or at school and can't come until nighttime or Saturday to kidnap you. Even if you ate your dad's Fair entry by mistake.

When Penny and I go back in, Coop wags and jumps around as if we've been gone a week. Mom is still on the phone.

My sister gets a piece of lined paper from the shelf and sits down at the table with a pencil. I need to go up to my room and check two important things in the Fair handbook before we go over to the fairgrounds. But first I want to be sure my sister has finished her oral report of the afternoon's events in general, and snack time in particular. So I hover in the hall doorway.

"Daddy brought my entries to the Fair already. I need you to help me write a list of them so I can count up how many prize ribbons to make space for on my bulletin board," Penny says. She's obviously talking to me, since Mom is busy.

I have really had enough of my sister for today—and maybe the rest of the year—but I sit down and take the pencil from her.

"Hey!" she yells. She snatches the pencil back.

Mom glances up from her conversation and gives me the warning eye.

"I thought you wanted me to make you a list," I say to Penny, trying for a nice-ish voice.

"No, I want to do it."

I make a face. When my sister writes, she uses what her teacher calls "inventive spelling." Her writing looks not so much like words or sentences, but more like what you'd get if you picked random letters out of a bag and scattered them along the tracks of a roller coaster. She always insists on having a helper sit with her and stare at the paper while she sounds out the words and prints them one painful letter at a time. When she's done, you have to "read" it, which is impossible. So she reads it for you.

After about sixteen centuries, Mom is still on the phone and my sister's Fair list is finished. It says:

> One sowd doll blankit one kla pig one drawing of Me riding on a hors that is runing threw a feeld of Star fish and cotten can<u>dy</u> trees one foto of <u>My</u> stuffd animals haveing a tee par<u>ty</u> one jar of pare butter.

"You didn't make pear butter," I say.

"My *class* did," Penny tells me as if she feels sorry for me because I'm so dense. "I can show you where my part is when I show you the jar tomorrow at the Fair."

I don't want to waste my breath trying to convince her that there's no such thing as one person's part of a group jar of pear butter, so I do what seems like the responsible thing and leave the room. Cooper follows me upstairs. If I get to be on my own at the Fair tomorrow, an extra great bonus will be that I'll be on the other side of the fairgrounds when Penny delivers her loud explanation about pear butter parts.

As soon as we get to my room, the Wonderdog lies down in his regular spot in the exact geometric middle of my floor. I step over him, take out my clay model of "The

Theory of Everything," and set it on my desk next to my bendable Albert Einstein. I always think about how Albert Einstein was working on a Theory of Everything a long time ago, even when he was sick and couldn't get out of bed anymore and some people thought he was a little past his brilliance expiration date. Which he wasn't.

I open my Fair handbook to the youth exhibit section. At the top, in bold letters, it says that if you had hands-on help from an adult you have to attach a note about it or your entry might be disqualified. My parents haven't even seen my project yet so I don't have to write anything about help. I flip to the page about sculptures. The first rule is that a sculpture can't be made of clay poured into a mold and baked because then it would be called ceramic, not sculpture. I am not sure what they mean by molds, and anyway I used modeling clay, which would melt into a disgusting puddle if you baked it and maybe even give off poison gas and then we'd have to evacuate the neighborhood.

There are more rules about sculptures, but I don't finish reading them because my sister walks into my room without knocking. As usual. Cooper's tail thumps because he doesn't know any better.

"I finished five things and they're already at the Fair. You didn't even finish one yet," Penny observes. "Want me to help you?"

"Not really," I say. I put the Fair handbook down so both of my hands will be free for project protection.

"What are those?" she says. She steps over Coop and points to the first three clay sculptures in my model.

I put a guarding hand in front of her pointing finger. "This one's a rock, this one's a beetle, and this one's a person," I tell her.

"What are they there for?"

I look at the ceiling. The last thing I want to do is explain the Theory of Everything to the Most Annoying Sister in the Galaxy, but while I'm examining my stick-on, glow-in-the-dark constellations it occurs to me that if *she* understands my model, then everyone else at the Fair will, too. Then maybe I'll win a blue ribbon, which would be great because I worked really hard on my sculpture.

"I can explain the whole project if you want," I offer.

Penny hops up onto my bed. She swings her legs. "Goody," she says. "Like we're playing school."

"So here's a rock and a beetle and a person," I start out.

"Those don't look like a rock and a beetle and a person," she says.

This is not going to be worth it, I think. But I go on.

"So we're going to zoom in on a rock, or a beetle, or a person, and take a look at its parts."

My sister holds up her hand.

"Yes, like your hand is a part of you," I say.

"No," she whispers so the other students who don't exist won't hear her. "I'm raising my hand. You have to call on me."

I can see that playing school with Penny is going to be more about her interrupting than about what I'm trying to teach.

"I can't call on you," I tell her, making up rules as I go. A scene from a movie I just saw pops into my mind.

"We're playing college, so this is a big classroom with a hundred students. I'm a professor and I'm giving a lecture. That means you have to sit and listen without talking, and write down everything I say. Get it?" I hand her a pad and a pencil.

She thinks about this for a couple of seconds. "I don't know."

I don't know why I bother to keep going, but I do. "Okay," I say. "So if you look closer at this rock there are parts you can see, like the different colored minerals." I show her the arrows pointing to the colored layers in my clay sculpture of a rock.

She makes a bunch of scribbles on the pad.

"Then if you want to look at smaller parts, you'd use strong microscopes to see the separate molecules of that mineral. You'd have to use even better and stronger scopes to see the individual atoms that go together to make the molecules, then you'd have to use even more powerful machines to see the parts of the atoms—the protons and neutrons and maybe even electrons that make up each atom."

I point to my clay models of the smaller and smaller particles I'm telling her about, one by one. I've pinned them under canning jar rings covered in plastic wrap. These are supposed to represent microscope lenses, which I now see requires a pretty good imagination.

"Can I play with Albert Einstein?" she asks.

"No," I say. "You're in college, remember?"

She scowls.

"Anyway," I tell her, "I'm getting to the good part now. Protons and neutrons are made of even smaller particles called quarks, and electrons are quarks, too, which brings us to—*tun-ta-da-taaaah!*—the Theory of Everything!"

Coop wags his tail because particle physics is fun. Penny looks skeptical. "I don't think college teachers sing like that," she says.

"Yes, they do," I say, wondering what I'm talking about. "Because they're excited about the strings."

I race through the rest of the explanation without stopping for a breath. "So, scientists think that the smallest particle everything is made of is not a particle at all, but is actually a teeny tiny loop of string. The best thing about the Theory of Everything is that *everything*—not just atoms, but even something like the force of gravity—is made of these subatomic strings. The strings can vibrate in lots of different ways"—here I wiggle my fingers to try and demonstrate what vibrate means—"and the different ways they vibrate is what adds up to a rock or a beetle or a person and even explains how the entire universe works!"

Now I'm standing up, holding my project and grinning at my sister. "Cool, right?"

Penny gets down off the bed. "No," she says. "It's dumb because your clay person looks like a lumpy toad." She pokes Albert Einstein with her finger on her way out. "Why don't you stick him on the corkboard?"

Albert falls over on his face. I set him upright because he's my favorite. I consider that sticking Pain-elope on the corkboard would solve some of my problems, but might also create a few new ones.

I go back to my model. I couldn't figure out how to make gravity or string theory strings out of clay, so I just explained those things on a card at the bottom of my project board. I'm pretty sure that physicists use math, not clay, to show how gravity and string theory strings work.

I stare at Albert Einstein.

Why don't you stick him on the corkboard?

This is actually not a bad idea. I take my modeling clay sculpture of a person off the board and carefully pin Albert Einstein there instead. He looks smart and interesting and nothing like a toad.

Next, I replace the clay blob rock with the chunk of feldspar dotted with garnet I found hiking on the ridge last week, using my glue gun to stick it on. After a minute, I jiggle my project. The feldspar stays put. So does Albert Einstein and everything else. Last year, when I entered my origami animal diorama, I found out that you will get a "nice try" ribbon if you just arrange things in place without fastening them on. Also, your project will go on display with all of its parts in a heap on the bottom.

I get rid of the clay beetle sculpture and take out the dead June bug I've been saving in my top desk drawer. One of its wing covers is gone, but there is no question about its beetleness. I attach it, too. Albert, the feldspar, and the real insect are big improvements.

I look over the rest of my model, then I go and get the family crafts box from the dining room cupboard. The Wonderdog follows me downstairs, then back up to my room. I jazz up the subatomic particle sculptures with buttons and yarn and sequins. I glue on some strands from a brand-new, shiny gold pom-pom bow so they look like wiggling loops. They work great for the string theory strings.

When I'm done, my project looks like a giant Theory of Everything party invitation. I wonder if it also looks like a blue-ribbon winner.

Thinking about winning first place reminds me of the other important thing I wanted to look up in the Fair handbook. I'm just opening to the adult baking page when I hear a knock on my door.

3
THE BLACK HOLE OF HOPPING

I don't need X-ray vision to know who is at my bedroom door. Painy never knocks, and my dad won't be back until we all come home together from the fairgrounds later tonight—a fact that would have been more useful to know *before* I fed everyone his Fair entry for snack. I close the Fair handbook and lower it to my side with my finger stuck in the adult baking page.

"Come on in, Mom," I say.

"I'm sorry to be in such a rush tonight, honey," she says, patting Cooper's shovelhead because it happens to be under her hand. "My phone won't stop ringing, and we have to get our entries over to the Fair before the seven o'clock deadline."

By "entries," she means my entry and my dad's entry. My entry is now ready. My dad's entry is the reason I was just about to check the rules in the Fair handbook. I wait, hoping her phone will ring again so she'll go back downstairs. It doesn't.

"Let's talk about our plan for the Fair tomorrow," Mom says, taking a seat on my bed.

The new plan! Thoughts fly around in my brain like spaceships launching into orbit. *Do I get to be on my own? What was the old plan? Is the new plan better? Or worse?*

One thought travels downstairs to the kitchen, where it peeks under a certain piece of aluminum foil. I slide the Fair handbook behind me, micron by micron, hoping it looks like I'm not moving at all. I need to be extra careful about what I do and say next, since that could tip the balance from a good Fair Friday plan to a bad Fair Friday plan.

"P-plan?" I stammer. *Brilliant start.*

"Dad and I arranged our volunteer shifts at the Fair so we could take turns being with you and Penny," Mom explains.

So *that's* the new plan? I still have to stay with a parent no matter how responsible I've been for weeks? Or days? Or at least all of today?

"But, Mom, I—"

"I have to work tomorrow, Miller," Mom says, as if I wasn't in the middle of a protest. "I may not make it to the Fair at all. I'm very disappointed. Now Dad will have to fill my volunteer shifts *and* his. He'll be working at one booth or another straight through the day. That's why we're changing the plan."

I sit up straight. So we're changing the bad plan? Could this mean what I hope it means—that tomorrow will be the best day of my whole life after all? I remove my finger from the adult baking page and let the Fair handbook slip behind me onto the floor. Why mention my mistake and tip the balance back again? I'm sure I can figure out how to fix the pie problem the same way I fixed my own Fair project—without adult help. I smile hugely and responsibly.

"It's okay, Mom," I tell her. "I can handle it. You can count on me."

"That's good, honey. I—"

"MOMMY!" Penny bursts into the room holding my mom's cell phone at arm's length like it's a bomb about to explode. "Of Ice is on the phone!"

Mom pats her empty pocket. "Penelope," she says, "you're not supposed to answer my calls." She stands up and reaches around Cooper for the cell phone, which he's busy snuffling.

"I didn't," my sister says. "I let the music play and play. Now I'm reading—see?" She points to the phone's screen. "Of Ice."

"Oh, *office*," Mom reads from the phone. "I'd better call back." She hurries out of my room. Coop lopes after her, because when he's not sleeping or having his belly rubbed he likes to follow the action.

Penny hops on one foot twice, then the other twice. "Of ice. Of ice," she chants. "How long—*hop hop*—do you think—*hop hop*—I can hop?"

Since being responsible is working out so well for me, I decide not to say my answer—"until your leg falls off"—out loud.

She balances on one foot. "I'm going to win first prize at the hopping contest tomorrow. You can cheer for me." She starts up again, twice on one foot, then twice on the other. "Of ice. Of ice..."

"There is no hopping contest at the Fair. And anyway, I'm..." All of my triumph about tomorrow gets sucked into the black hole that has formed around the hopping going on in my room. I feel my breath coming faster and faster. If neither of our parents can be with us at the Fair, then who is going to take care of—?

"MOM!" I hurtle to the top of the stairs. "If you and Dad aren't going to take her, then who's going to be at the Fair with Penny?"

My mom is still talking on the phone and doesn't answer me. Penny hops out of my room and down the stairs one step at a time, holding onto the banister.

"The same person—*hop*—who's going to—*hop*—take care of you, of course," she says over her shoulder. "Andrew's—*hop*—mommy."

4
SHIFTING MOLECULES

I can't argue my mom out of her newer and horribler Holmsbury Fair plan because she's still talking on the phone. While I'm waiting for her to finish, I go to the basement to find a box so I can pack up my redecorated Theory of Everything sculpture. I bring the box back to my room and look over my project one more time. Albert Einstein is pinned to the board, ready to go to the Fair with his favorite friends, the quarks and the strings. I have to spend my Fair Friday with Andrew, his mother, and Painy. With a sad shake of my head, I slide my project into the box and set it down on the bed.

On to my next problem. I retrieve the Fair handbook from the floor. In big, bold letters at the top of the adult baking's pie section it says that each entry "must be a whole, uncut pie in its original dish."

Not good, I think.

On the plus side, what's left of the pie is in its original dish. I can't find anything at all in the Fair handbook about accidental eating.

"Miller, we have to head over to the fairgrounds now," Mom calls from downstairs. "Bring a sweatshirt."

Penny flings open my door and yells, "WE HAVE TO GO NOW!" as if I'm not standing four feet away from her. "BRING A SWEATSHIRT!"

I put the Fair handbook down. Maybe I can get the adult baking judges to take my dad's pie anyway. I tie my "Physicists are Quarky" sweatshirt around my waist and carry my project downstairs. My mom's in the kitchen, frowning while she writes on her notepad.

"Miller, would you please put your entry in the car and then come back for Dad's pie?" she asks.

I go out and set my project box on the backseat of the car so I can hold onto it while we're driving. I open the trunk, then go back into the house for what's left of the pie.

"Penny, you can go and get into the car," Mom says. "I'll be right out."

"What about Miller?" Penny points at me just in case our mom isn't sure who I am. "He needs to get in the car, too."

"Yes, Miller and I will both be right out."

From the doorsill, Mom watches Penny get into the car. When she turns to me, I stop wondering about leaving my sister alone in the car with my project because the look on

Mom's face has moved into the red zone of the serious-meter. *Uh-oh.* We're going to have a Talk, and it is probably going to be about pie. Right away I feel a quadrillion molecules of sorry form inside me, because that's what happens when we have a Talk. Even if I didn't eat the pie on purpose, and I didn't eat it all myself. I could have, though, because it was the best ever. Which is why we weren't supposed to eat it in the first place, I guess.

"Miller—" Mom says.

"Mom," I start to explain, "I really—"

She holds up her hand to stop me.

This is not normal, because before today my mom has always heard me out. Even if *I* interrupt *her*, like I just did.

"I don't want Penny out there in the car by herself, so I'd like you to listen for now, okay?" She looks out the window while she's saying this.

I gulp a few times. "Okay," I croak. Eating my dad's lemon meringue pie has apparently put me in new and unexplored Talk territory. Cooper pushes his big head under my hand, which always makes me feel better, especially right now.

"I'm going to drop you two off at the candy apple tent with Dad. He's jammed up and still has a couple of other booths to wire. I probably won't be home until very late—after you're in bed. Here's some money for dinner for you and Penny."

I take the folded-up bills from her. I take a breath. So far this doesn't seem like a Talk. And so far, nothing about the pie. Some of my molecules of sorry transform back into regular ones.

Mom reaches over and cups my chin. "Since you've become so grown-up and responsible lately, I want to explain why I have to miss our special night-before-the-Fair family time."

If my mom considers me grown-up and responsible at this particular moment then she can't know about the pie. A few of my regular molecules shift into hopeful ones. I try to stop glancing at the top of the refrigerator.

But if my mom considers me grown-up and responsible, *why, oh why* does she still want to ruin what was going to be the best day of my life, by making me stay with Andrew's mother tomorrow? Lewis is right. My mom's logic is impossible to follow.

"Mom," I start. "About tomorrow...can't I just—"

"A serious emergency came up at work this afternoon," Mom says, holding up her hand again. She takes a deep breath. "A young teenager is missing from her group home."

This pushes all thoughts of the Fair out of my mind. I know from my mom that some of the teens in her program live with their families and some don't. The ones that don't live at home sometimes live with foster families, or they live in group homes with other teenagers and with adults who help them. But I never heard about one of them going missing.

"Maybe she's just at the store or something," I think, out loud.

"Maybe," Mom says. She smiles in a sad way that tells me she wishes my idea could be right but knows it isn't.

"She'll come back, though," I say, "because even a teenager can't take care of herself all the time, right?" Then I remember that my mom asked me to listen, so I don't offer any other helpful comments like that.

"A thirteen-year-old girl should not be all on her own," Mom says. She frowns at the phone. "Lots of people are looking for her, and I need to help." She hugs me and kisses the top of my head. "Thank you for being so careful, Miller," she says.

Careful not to go missing?

"Mo-o-o-mmmm!" Penny shrills from the car.

"I'm coming, sweetheart."

I look out the window, then at Mom. Maybe teenagers have gone missing before now and I just wasn't old enough to know about them. Mom's worry lines are as deep as I've ever seen them, and that's saying a lot.

She points to the top of the fridge. "Don't forget Dad's lemon meringue pie." She smiles, and raises both hands with all of her fingers crossed in a gesture that means *I hope he wins first place!*

I smile and raise my hands with my fingers crossed back at her in a gesture that means *I hope the judges don't notice that seven-eighths of the pie is missing!*

I'm not going to talk to Mom about missing pie when

she's already using so much of her worry energy for that missing girl. And even though I have to clamp my mouth shut to do it, I stop myself from asking to be on my own at the Fair, too. I wonder if this is me being responsible and careful, but I'm not too sure.

I slide the dish off the fridge. I stare at the foil and wish my mom could have this last piece of lemon meringue pie I saved for her. I wish there was another perfect and whole pie to enter. But mostly I wish that tonight would just be the same for us as every other Thursday night before the Fair—my family walking around together in the quiet dark, eating our first Fair food supper and checking out all of the closed-up booths that are waiting for the morning, same as we are. I let out a long breath, get my dad's entry form from the side of the fridge, and say "see ya" to Coop as I go out the door.

There's a blanket in the trunk, and I kind of scrunch it up and set the blue pie dish in the middle of it so the pie won't slide around. Maybe I should just let the dish slide, and then I could blame the car ride for the pie's current condition. But a one-slice pile of glop can't turn into a whole pie's worth of glop, no matter how much the pie's molecules shift around or how wildly its subatomic strings vibrate and wiggle in the trunk of a car. I tuck the blanket around the dish.

After I close the trunk, I slide into the backseat and pull my project box onto my lap. Penny is staring out the window and humming. That missing girl is still on my mind,

but now so is the missing pie. I'm hoping that the saying "out of sight, out of mind" will hold true regarding my sister's mind when it comes to the pie. Hopefully Penny's mind won't zigzag from hopping to Fair ribbons to lemon meringue during our three-and-a-half-minute car ride to the fairgrounds. But in the random world of my sister's thoughts, it could definitely happen.

5
JOKES ON MY PLANET

The three-and-a-half-minute ride to the Holmsbury fairgrounds feels like three and a half years. This is because Penny makes up a counting song about all of the food booths she wants to eat at tonight and sings it over and over while holding up counting fingers right in front of my face. I've been to the fairgrounds on Thursday night enough times to know that the Holmsbury Helping Hands Club and the high school's SportsBoosters are the only food booths that will be open. In the hopes of stopping the entertainment, I mention this to my sister.

"They changed it this year," she informs me.

"No they didn't."

"Yes they did. Lou-Ann told me that today."

Just as I start to ask how Lou-Ann could have told her anything today since she never seems to talk, we turn onto the fairgrounds. So instead, I stick my head out of the car.

This way at least one part of me is somewhere my six-year-old sister isn't.

Mom winds our car slowly down the paved Fair path. The sun is sinking behind the trees at the bottom of the hill and the tents glow like they're lit from inside with sunset. Strings of colored flag triangles ripple and snap in the breeze. The truck in front of us stops at every booth, and high school kids jump off of the back delivering huge pots of mums for decoration.

In front of our car, people cross the path in fifty-three directions. Some of them have entries in boxes or wagons, and some are hauling carts of food for the booths. Most of them wave at my mom or me or my sister, or just at our car because they know us. Tomorrow there'll be no cars on these paths, just people. During the Fair, Mom can't walk three steps along here without stopping to chat with someone she knows. Dad always smiles and inches off in the direction of the burger he hasn't eaten yet, or the band he wants to hear, but my Mom's million hellos are part of what makes the Fair ours.

Way down the hill, the Ferris Wheel is turning. I can't wait to see my eleven-and-a-half-year-old view of the whole Fair and even all of Holmsbury. The Fair's force field is practically pulling me out of the car.

"More booths will be open—you'll see," Penny says, turning her already impressive volume up. "Especially the *dessert* ones."

My brain alarm goes off. I duck my head back into the car.

She says, "Tonight, for dessert, since I already had lem—"

"LOOK!" I shout at the top of my lungs. "There's Dad!" I reach across Penny and wave out of her window. "Dad! Dad!"

"Mmmph!" Penny says, since my shoulder is blocking her mouth.

My dad is crouched in the shadows next to the high school's striped candy apple tent. Two other parents are leaning over him holding big silver flashlights. He twists his head sideways and grins at us, then goes back to his work. Our car bumps onto the grass in front of the tent.

"Let's go, kids," Mom says. "Miller, why don't you get your things out of the car? I have to talk to Dad for a quick minute before I leave. Penny, you come with me."

I hug my project box to my chest and stand still, letting the Fair swirl around me. Carousel music coming from the midway mixes with voices and hammering and engine noises and the buzz of power tools. I can already smell fried dough and barbecue smoke. I watch people hurry from one booth to another like electrons jumping between atoms. Prickles of nighttime air give me goose bumps, so I put my sweatshirt on.

I open the trunk and peek under the foil. Even the power of the Fair's force field could not create missing pie matter out of thin air. Looking at the almost-empty dish sucks some of the energy out of the air around me. I put the pie dish and my dad's entry form on top of my project box and close the trunk.

"All set?" Mom asks, coming over. "Penny's already helping Dad."

Next to the candy apple tent, my sister is waving the wide end of one of those big silver flashlights dangerously close to Dad's forehead. That could be considered helping, if he wants a concussion. But if she *is* "helping" Dad, then I can turn in his entry without her.

"It's all right with Dad if you drop off the entries on your own," Mom says, sounding like it's not exactly all right with her. "But—" Her phone rings again.

"Hello?" She listens for a couple of seconds. "Oh, I see. You think she might have gone *where?*" Mom's voice goes up about an octave. She glances at me, and then at Penny, as if she's making sure we haven't gone off somewhere crazy ourselves. We haven't.

I lean my back against the car and look down the hill. The dairy cattle barn is right at the bottom, and I can see shapes of people moving around just inside the big open doors. I wonder if Bailey, from my class at school, is down at the barn with her prize-winning cow, Cosette. The symbol of the Holmsbury Fair is a black-and-white cow, so all of the black-and-white cows are practically celebrities. I think Cosette won Best in Show last year for the cows, which is really hard for a cow to do.

The actual Fair mascot is a seventh-grader's father who sort of waltzes around in a cow suit. The only thing worse than being in sixth grade and still having to stay with your parents might be getting to be on your own, then spending all day trying to avoid your dad, the dancing cow.

"I know. Okay. No, I'll come pick you up," Mom says. "I'm on my way. Thanks." She drops her phone into her open purse.

"I'm so sorry that I have to go," she tells me. "I wanted us to be together tonight, like we've always been." She points to the wide-open, garage-sized door of the youth exhibit that's only about fifteen steps down the hill. "I didn't want you to go off by yourself…but I guess it should be okay." She doesn't sound convinced. "Take your entry down there, then come right back up to the adult baking exhibit with Dad's pie."

The long white building at the far end of our row of food tents and booths is for adult baking. A line of people holding boxes and plates stretches partway down the hill from its door.

"When you're done, please go and find Dad," Mom says. "If he's finished at the candy apple tent he'll be at the elementary school's corn stand. He'll need help with Penny." She gives me a quick hug, gets into the car, and pulls onto the Fair path. The car stops. "The corn stand is at the end of the next row, two-thirds of the way up the hill," she calls out, as if it hasn't been in the same place every year since, oh, forever. I want to tell her that I promise that I won't go missing, but I don't think that will help her worry any less. So I don't.

I walk down the hill to the youth exhibit by myself. This would be a lot more fun if I didn't have to worry about what'll happen when I'm done there and have to go try and enter my dad's pie in adult baking. Inside the youth building entries are piled every which way on tables, chairs, and on the floor. Crafts, home-grown vegetables, cooking, artwork—you name it, someone entered it. By tomorrow morning at nine o'clock every single entry will be hanging up or set on a shelf or arranged in some kind of display that looks good enough to be in a museum. Only it's better than a museum, because there are prize ribbons, too. I hope this year's judges like molecules and quarks and strings.

One of the check-in volunteers calls out, "Please hand us your entry form first."

Entry form?

My dad's entry form for adult baking is sticking out from under the pie dish. I know exactly what's on it: his name, address, phone number, and age. In the category space he's printed "pie," and next to the variety space are the words "lemon meringue." I picture the bulletin board in my room where *my* entry form is still pinned. My name, address, phone number, and age are printed on it. The category space is blank, because I didn't finish filling it out.

"Guh," I say. I lean against the edge of a table piled as high as my shoulders with filled-in forms.

"What's up, Miller?"

I almost drop my box *and* the pie plate. I didn't notice Mrs. Noyes behind the entry form tower. Mrs. Noyes, who is in charge of the youth exhibit, is the nicest grown-up in the Fair and maybe in the world, which I found out last year when I picked up my diorama. She told me that my origami animals were really "first-place fantastic" and that I should try using a glue gun next time if I could, because the judges want everything firmly attached. "Those judges are sticklers for rules," she told me, which according to her is why they gave me the "nice try" ribbon.

Now she even remembers my name and it's a whole year later. She is peering at me over her half glasses, waiting for me to tell her why I groaned.

"I left my entry form on my bulletin board," I tell her.

"Do you have time to go home and get it?"

My mom drove away a few minutes ago and my dad is trying not to get his head split open by a flashlight. I can't run home and back and still get both entries in by seven o'clock. So I shake my head no.

Mrs. Noyes looks over her glasses at the line of people. She keeps her eyes on everyone else and at the same time slides something next to my box. It's a blank entry form.

"You didn't get it from me," she says, making the words come out of the side of her mouth.

I thank her out of the side of my mouth, then scrunch down to fill out my new form.

When it's my turn to check in, the entry-taker, who's also the lunch lady from the elementary school, tries to take my dad's pie. She does this even though I already handed her my new form that says "sculpture" right on it and I'm pretty sure a pie is not a sculpture. I keep a tight hold on the dish.

"That's not my entry," I say, but it's too late because she's already peeking underneath a corner of the aluminum foil.

"I guess not," she laughs, "since it's almost eaten up. Looks good, though. Can I have that last bite—ha ha?"

I'm not sure how to answer. If I say no then I'm sort of being rude. But if I say yes and go along with her joke, I might end up with no pie at all. So instead of answering, I stand there and stare over her head like no one tells jokes on my planet.

After the silence has stretched into a reasonable six years or so, she asks, "Is your sculpture in that box?"

"Yes," I say. I set everything down on the table and take the pie dish off of my project box. The lunch lady peers inside the box at the Theory of Everything.

She looks from my new entry form to my project and back again and says, "This isn't a sculpture."

I wonder if the modeling clay parts are harder to notice, now that it's more of a Theory of Everything party invitation. The opening of the box isn't facing me, so I can't point things out. "There's a modeling clay molecule there," I tell her. "And an atom, too."

"I see them, but this still won't qualify as a sculpture."

I picture all of the brand-new decorations and realistic additions to my project. I wince. Earlier this afternoon I thought they were better parts, but I didn't stop to think about the fact that because those things aren't clay they're *different* kinds of parts. Changing some of the parts has made it into a whole different project.

"Would it have been a sculpture if the bug and the rock and everything was made of modeling clay?" I ask, waiting for the bad news.

"Nope," she says. "A sculpture is one item, all in one piece."

Well, at least I didn't wreck it with Albert Einstein. I'm a little relieved. But not a lot.

She shows me the Fair handbook where it says that a sculpture has to be all in one piece. She's pointing to the place where I had to stop reading when my sister barged into my room earlier today to "help" me.

"Can I enter it as something else?" I ask.

"Sure," the lunch lady says. "We can just change it on your form."

Now I'm a lot relieved. If my project isn't a sculpture because it has lots of different pieces, maybe it'll do better as a diorama, since this year the pieces are securely attached.

"Can it be a diorama?"

"Sorry." She shakes her head. "Rule number one for dioramas is that they have to be in a shoe box."

"Oh. Right." I look down at her copy of the Fair handbook, open to the youth exhibit rules. "Do you have a category called physics?"

"Ha ha." She laughs again.

I guess we do tell jokes on my planet.

Just not on purpose.

"We'll find something." She skims through the category list, tracing her finger under each line. "Gift made of natural materials? No. Creative use of recycled materials?" She raises one eyebrow at me.

I consider this. It does seem like everything on the board, even Albert Einstein, was used for something else first. All of the parts could add up to creative use of recycled materials. That sounds good. Then I remember that the extra fancy string-theory bow was brand-new with a price tag on it before I cut it up.

"It's not *all* recycled," I admit.

"Well, the judges are sticklers," the lunch lady warns me.

"I know," I say.

"Let's see." She continues looking through the categories. "Knitting—no. Pottery—no. Not woodworking, either. Hmm...how about collections?" She smiles up at me. "A physics collection! What do you think?"

I think my Theory of Everything project isn't really a collection, like a bunch of animal-shaped erasers would be, or pennies from the 1900s that have been run over by trains. But I can see by her page-skimming finger that we're pretty much at the end of the list. And I can see by the clock on the wall that if I don't make it to the adult baking building soon, it will close. If that happens, I might as well have given her the last slice of lemon meringue pie after all.

"Okay," I sigh. "A collection." I change the form.

She makes a big check mark on it and hands me a receipt.

"Good luck!" she says. She puts my project box on the table full of entries behind her, then shouts, "Next!"

I wonder if I should have checked my project over once more before turning it in. I say a silent good-bye to my Theory of Everything collection and pick up the pie dish. If I want to be on my own at the Fair tomorrow, I'll need a lot more than luck at my next stop.

6
ONE-EIGHTH RELIEVED, SEVEN-EIGHTHS WORRIED

At three minutes to seven I am the only person left in line at the adult baking check-in. With me I have one entry form, one-eighth of a pie, and zero brilliant ideas for what to do about it.

The guy sitting at the check-in table stands up. I recognize him because when he's not a member of the adult baking committee he's Mr. Hansen, the owner of Hansen's Hardware. He shapes his hands into a megaphone and aims it at the back of the building.

"I'M SHUTTING THE DOORS," he booms. "GET READY TO MOVE THE ENTRIES!"

He pushes and pulls at the sliding barn doors behind me, making a *scree-ee-eek* like a sound effect in a horror movie. This would make good background noise for one of Lewis's projects. When the doors bang together, Mr. Hansen drops a heavy board across the inside into two big hooks.

I'm locked in adult baking.

"We close up at seven," he tells me. "That's the rules. I'm just making sure yours is the last entry." He wipes his face with a handkerchief, then looks at my dish. "Just one? Great!"

He's glad there's only one piece of pie in the dish? This *is* great! After a second it dawns on me that he can't actually see through the foil. What he means by "great!" is that he's glad I only have one entry for him to check in.

Maybe I can tell him that this is a new, single-serving kind of pie. Or that mathematically, one-eighth could count as a whole if that's all you have. But the words sound so dumb in my head that I don't let them come out of my mouth. I set the heavy dish down on the table and hand over my dad's entry form without saying anything.

Mr. Hansen looks over the form and makes a quick check after every line. "Mm-hmm." *Check.* "Mm-hmm." *Check.* "Lemon meringue..." He scrawls a label on a piece of tape and sticks it to the side of the foil. "You're all set." He stands up.

All set? The lunch lady looked my project over before she took it in to make sure it followed the rules. If Mr. Hansen takes the pie without looking, does that mean it's in the Fair, even if it doesn't follow the rules? I'm one-eighth relieved, but still seven-eighths worried.

"Wait a minute." He glances at the form and then at me.

"Sanford? You're Rob Sanford's kid? I thought you looked familiar. He's something, your dad. Never says much, always wins big. I've got to get a look at his pie!"

The fact that you know almost everybody who volunteers at the Holmsbury Fair is normally part of what makes it so great. Now I watch Mr. Hansen reach for the foil and hope a wormhole will appear and whoosh me through the fabric of space-time to some other part of the fairgrounds in some other year, even if it's a year when I'm a hundred and still have never been to the Fair by myself.

"HANSEN!" someone shouts from the far end of the building. "We need you down here!"

"Okay, okay!" Mr. Hansen takes my dad's unpeeked-at pie slice and slides it into the last empty space on the loaded shelves behind him. Then he gathers up a huge mess of entry forms.

Whew! My dad's pie is on the shelf, so I guess it's entered. Now I just want to get out of here. The door is still barred. I try to make the two-by-four levitate out of its hooks by mental telepathy, which doesn't work.

"If you don't mind having a seat for a minute"—Mr. Hansen waves his fistful of forms toward a bench—"I'll be right back to let you out. Can't open the doors just yet or we'd get people showing up with late entries and we'd be here all night." Mr. Hansen hurries away.

"It's not so bad to be here all night." A tall, skinny man I didn't notice before has appeared next to me. He looks like he is a hundred years old. "When I was a boy," he says, folding himself down onto the bench, "we camped out to guard the Fair."

"That sounds fun." I bet they probably went to the Fair all day by themselves, too.

"Guarding the Fair was a lot more fun than cleaning up after the cow parade they used to have down Main Street—also our job." He chuckles. "Everyone calls me Rip. How about you?"

"I'm Miller," I tell him.

"New in town?"

"No, I was born here, Mr. Rip," I say.

"Not Mister," he corrects me. "Just Rip."

Mr. Hansen returns from the back with a crew of helpers. "I'll let you out in just another minute," he tells me. "Cakes first," he calls to the committee members.

They grab layer cakes, Bundt cakes, and fancy decorated cakes and take them to the back.

I glance at my dad's pie on the shelf. Even if it goes all the way through to the judging, I am pretty sure that the sticklers-for-rules judges aren't going to give him first place for one-eighth of a pie sitting in a plate full of crumbs. He's never gotten anything less than a second. Do they even give "nice try" ribbons in this exhibit if you break the rules? I swallow hard.

I realize that Rip is watching me. I make myself turn away from the pies.

He looks me over from head to sneakers. "What are you, eleven?" he asks.

I nod, because I don't think the "and-a-half" part matters to someone who's a hundred.

"Eleven still counts as new in town, Milton," Rip informs me.

"It's Miller," I say. "My dad's great-grandmother used to live here. My dad visited a lot when he was little."

I want to tell this man that growing from a baby to a nursery-schooler to a kindergartner, and then all the way up to a sixth-grader in the same house on the same street in the same town isn't exactly new. But I don't. Instead, I ask, "How long do you have to live here *not* to be new?"

"Long enough to remember when it cost a kid a dime to get into the Fair."

"Wow," I say. That must be a pretty long time ago, since now it costs five dollars.

"And long enough to have snuck in through a hole in the old graveyard fence when you didn't have the dime," he adds. He looks over his shoulder, then lowers his voice. "I did it once, on a dare. Was about your age, too, Milo," he says.

"Quick breads are next," Mr. Hanson instructs the crew.

I shoot another look at my dad's pie.

Rip leans in close so I have to pay attention. "But one of the Maynards grabbed me right as I was going through the fence." He swipes at the air with his long, knobby fingers.

"Who are the Maynards?" I ask.

He raises his eyebrows. "The *Maynards*. Those sisters who refused to get married because they didn't want to be separated from each other. They were buried all in a row in the old graveyard. The stones are decorated with flying death heads. It was around the 1730s, I think."

Flying death heads? "Wait—*buried* in the 1730s? You're saying a *ghost* grabbed you?" Now he's got my full attention.

"You don't know the story of the Maynards?" Rip says. "The three oldest sisters drowned when their carriage slid off the bridge and plunged into the icy Holmsbury River."

He glances side to side and lowers his voice. "Their driver drowned, too."

I can't imagine anyone drowning in the Holmsbury River. It's just a shallow creek that winds through our town park. I guess it must have been a lot deeper and wider back then.

"Pies!" Mr. Hansen shouts.

I jerk around to check the shelves so fast that I almost fall off the bench. The baking committee starts taking pies from the far end.

Now that I think about it, I'm pretty sure I've never seen a "nice try" ribbon in adult baking. I should've just told my dad we ate the pie. This is not going to end well. I start to breathe faster.

"Those three dead women still haunt the old graveyard looking for their youngest sister—the missing fourth one of the set," Rip continues. He pulls himself up to his full, rickety height. "Everybody knows that."

"I didn't," I admit, trying to keep an eye on the pies and listen at the same time.

"That's because you're new. Anyway"—Rip leans in again—"I got away from that Maynard sister. I ran straight up the hill and out the front gate of the Fair." He zooms his hand up and over my head like a plane taking off.

"Boy, there sure are a lot of pies this year," one of the committee members exclaims. She's looking right at our blue pie dish and another right next to it. "I'll have to come back for these last two." She takes two other pies and walks away.

I gulp. My dad is a great baker, and no matter how many pies there are, or how little pie is in his dish, he still deserves a blue ribbon for his lemon meringue. But when the baking committee looks under that foil, they'll call my dad and tell him that his pie is disqualified. I have to do something. Fast. My heart kicks up to double-time.

Rip doesn't seem to notice that I'm only half listening. "I kept on running from that grabbing ghost until I was all the way home," he goes on. "I sat myself down and wrote a note explaining how sorry I was for sneaking into the Fair, then I marched myself right back to the gate and dropped the note in the bucket, along with *two* dimes." He looks at me with a funny kind of smile. "They sure liked that note, Myron."

The end of Rip's story makes it seem more like a lesson about not sneaking into the Fair than a ghost story.

I'm watching the pie carriers walk toward the shelves again.

In my brain, Rip's sorry-I-snuck-in note bumps around with the I-had-help notes kids are supposed to write for the youth exhibit.

Sorry and help. Sorry and help.

Two dishes are left on the pie shelf, and one is ours. I feel like time is speeding up around me.

Sorry and help! I lurch to my feet and grab a piece of paper and a pencil from the check-in table. I dash out a note:

Dear Pie Judges:

I am really sorry that we tasted most of my dad's pie by mistake. Tasting was how we helped him, until today. He practiced and practiced, so I hope he can still be in the fair because this pie is his best ever, and that's saying a lot. One important fact is that this nice piece of pie is still in its original baking dish. Thank you.

Sincerely,
Miller Sanford

I glance around. Rip is gone. No one is near the shelves. I'll slip the note under the foil for the judges to read after I'm gone. They need to know that the missing pie is my fault, not my dad's, so letting them know that is the responsible thing to do. Even if the judges don't really want explaining notes in adult baking, they're sure to read it—unless I'm still here when they find it, in which case they might just hand the note back, and the pie with it. Ugh.

I take a step toward the blue dish.

There's a crash behind me. I whip around as Mr. Hansen takes the fallen two-by-four off of his foot. He moves it aside, then yanks one side of the creaky barn door open.

"Thanks for waiting," he tells me, rubbing his foot. He glances all around outside the open door. "No late bakers. All clear."

"Great," I say. "I...just...um..."

I turn back to the shelves. They're empty. I consider the note in my hand. At the other end of the building, every member of the adult baking committee is milling around the tables full of entries. There's no way to get the note into the pie dish without being seen now. I'm too late. All of the air leaks out of me as I crumple the note into my pocket.

Rip is standing just inside the doorway. "Off you go, now, Miller," he says. "Don't let the Maynard sisters catch you sneaking into the Fair!"

"I won't," I say. I'm not thinking about any old ghost stories now. I have to tell my dad that I ate a good hunk of his Fair entry and fed the rest to the neighborhood kids. Will he think I'm responsible after hearing that?

As soon as I step outside, the Fair's force field hits me with full power. Lots more lights have come on all around. Everything sparkles. The pathways are mostly empty and the tall lights have misty yellow rings around them like little Saturns. Down at the midway so many neon signs are flashing that the rides look like they're lit by fireworks. The carousel music is still coming up the hill through the cooling night air. I fill my insides with a big breath of Fair and giant-step along the row of food tents.

7
GHOST MATTER THEORIES

The candy apple tent is empty and dark, so I head up the hill to the Holmsbury Elementary School corn stand. My dad is crouching next to a metal pot on legs. It looks like a witch's cauldron, only it's silver, not black. It's big enough to boil at least thirty ears of corn. I'm so hungry I could eat ten of them myself, straight out of the pot. People who come to the Fair from other towns slop butter all over their corn because they don't know how delicious it is just plain. The serving table always gets slimed, and kids who are helping out have to wipe dripped butter off of it every other minute.

"Hi, Dad," I say.

"Ha-ah," Dad says, which is "hiya" with a penlight in his mouth. "Enchees ing?"

I'd better get it over with. "The entries are in, Dad, but—"

"I'm ready for din-ner!" Penelope singsongs from her perch on top of a stack of hay bales.

Dad points the penlight at me and makes it flash off and on with his teeth.

"Okay, okay, I get the message." I shield my eyes. "I'll take her." He's pretty busy, so I figure now's probably not the best time to tell him about his pie.

"Hanks. Hab fum." The light sweeps down my face and arcs back over to his wiring job.

"Let's go," I tell Penny.

She slides off the hay bales and we walk along the path toward the Holmsbury Helping Hands and Sportsboosters booths.

"Remember," she says, "there are lots of other food places open because Lou-Ann said—"

"Okay, fine." I make a ninety-degree turn and start down the hill. Walking around the shuttered-up Fair is one of my favorite things to do, so even though I'm hungry and we're not going to find open food booths anywhere else, I don't mind making a big Fair circle for nothing. Penny runs to catch up.

Partway down the hill we pass a bunch of grown-ups standing in the bed of a pickup truck. They're pushing and pulling on a pumpkin the size of a fat washing machine.

"Whoa, baby!" one of them yells.

"Easy there!" warns another.

The pumpkin teeters at the top of the ramp on the back of the pickup.

"Watch it!"

"LOOK OUT!"

The giant pumpkin decides to slide down the ramp without help. When it reaches the bottom it doesn't smash, which is good for the person who grew it, but bad if you were hoping to see the giant goo and giant seeds and whatever else might be inside.

"I want to go in there. Giant jack-o'-lanterns are fun!" Penny says. She tugs me over to the fence. It's dark and I see Lou-Ann's mother just in time not to walk straight into her. She's standing at the pumpkin patch gate.

"Hi, Miller. Hi, Penny," she says. "Sorry, but no one can go in while pumpkins are rolling."

"That's okay," I say. I turn to Penny. "These aren't giant jack-o'-lanterns, anyway," I tell her. "They're pumpkins that get weighed, not carved."

"Actually, we *are* having giant pumpkin carving this year," Lou-Ann's mother says. "The carvers are going to work all day tomorrow, and the winners will be announced around dinnertime."

Penny shoots me a giant told-you-so face. "We're getting dinner now," she tells Lou-Ann's mother.

"Better head up to SportsBoosters or Helping Hands, then," Lou-Ann's mother says. "Nothing else is open, and they'll probably close soon, too."

"Okay," Penny agrees, since this information has now

come from a reliable source, meaning anybody but me. "I want egg and cheese on a roll."

I spin on my heel, take her back up to SportsBoosters, and use the money my mom gave me to buy her an egg and cheese. I get one for my dad, too, smothered in ketchup the way he likes it. I buy Helping Hands clam chowder for me, and it isn't until we sit down at a picnic table and I put that first salty, potatoful taste of Fair in my mouth that I remember that the old guy in adult baking, Rip, finally called me Miller that last time he said my name. Not Milo, not Milton, and not Myron.

He knew my real name all along, I realize. Then I have to chew over everything else he said that might have been kidding or not kidding. Especially those things about ghosts in the old graveyard next to the fairgrounds.

As I take another spoonful of chowder, I consider possible scientific explanations for ghost matter. Maybe ghost matter could be made of neutrinos. Since neutrinos are real particles that move through space every nanosecond and even pass right through things like our bodies and the Earth without us seeing or feeling them, neutrinos seem like good ghost material. I wonder if anyone else has thought of this.

Penny starts to rock from side to side on the bench across from me but I ignore her. I have just realized that if the Maynard sister ghost was made of neutrinos, her neutrino fingers would have passed right through Rip. So how would he have known that she grabbed him? He wouldn't have felt anything at all, unless lots of neutrinos in one place *can* feel like something. And can neutrinos even be in the shape of fingers?

Penny clamps a hand over her mouth and giggles escape between her fingers, but I don't really care what she thinks is funny because I'm too busy wondering if the Theory of Everything could be used to explain something about ghosts. It stands to reason that if *everything*—even gravity, which is a force and not an actual, solid *thing*—is made of tiny vibrating strings, then if ghost matter existed it could be made of subatomic strings, too. Ghosts are supposed to be invisible, but gravity is real and it's definitely invisible, and that doesn't bother the scientists who work on string theory. What matters is how the strings vibrate. Ghost matter strings could vibrate so we can't see them, just like gravity strings do.

Then I come up with an even stranger theory about ghosts: what if the invisible parts of a person—like our thoughts and feelings—are somehow made of vibrating strings, too? What happens to those invisible thoughts-and-feelings strings after a person's body—the visible, solid, molecular part of a person—isn't alive anymore? Maybe *that's* what ghost matter would be, if there were such a thing.

I shift on the picnic bench to face in the direction of the old graveyard and *bam!* ghost matter theories disappear from my brain and I'm looking straight into the lens of Lewis's video camera.

Penny bounces up and down on the bench. "I didn't tell! I didn't tell!" she says. The whole table shakes.

Lewis gapes at Penny, then looks at me. "You're kidding! She didn't tell about the p—?"

"Pumpkins!"

I jolt into action, blabbing right over the word he's about to say, which is a word I don't want reinserted into my sister's brain. I need to tell my dad about the snack time disaster myself, not have Penny tell on me.

"Huh?" She stops bouncing and gives me a look.

"Pumpkins," I repeat. "Tell Lewis about the giant *pumpkin* carving!" I grin at Lewis with all of my teeth—which I realize probably looks more scary than cheery—and I'm nodding like one of those bobblehead dolls you win if you swing the Hammer Striker hard enough to ring the bell at the midway. I am going to look like a lunatic on Lewis's video.

"Mill, what're you talk—"

I kick him under the table. "PUMP-kins," I say again, widening my eyes in a signal I hope means *don't say pie!*

"Ow!" he says. "I mean...*oh*! Okay! Giant carved PUMP-kins. Really?"

"You are not talking about what I'm talking about!" Penny explodes. "Not pumpkins! I mean I didn't tell you that Lewis was here! You didn't see him making a movie of you, and I acted like I didn't see him to keep it a secret!"

"Pretty much," Lewis allows.

"And there *are* going to be giant jack-o'-lanterns," she adds. "I knew that, too, and Miller didn't."

I may not have known about the giant pumpkin carving, but I do know that I'm done talking about it. "You didn't tell me you were coming tonight," I say to Lewis.

"My brother let me come over because your parents are with you," he says. "Where are they, anyway? Why aren't you all together like usual?"

"My dad's still wiring the corn stand. And he has more to do, too. My mom had to go to her office so she can't be here at all."

"Too bad." Lewis turns his camera back on. "Hey, keep eating," he says. "This is a good shot with the 'World's Best Hot Fudge Sundae' sign behind you."

"But I already finished my egg and cheese," Penny tells him.

"That's okay." Lewis points the camera at her cheese-smeared face, clearly visible under the lights around the picnic tables.

I slurp in another spoonful of clams and potatoes. If I were on a far-off planet and some extraterrestrial being somehow gave me just one spoonful of this chowder, I'd know right off that it came from the Holmsbury Fair. Same with all of my favorite Fair foods. Tomorrow I'll start my day with a Community Pantry colossal sugar donut, then for midmorning snack, Firefighter fries. From there I'll move on to the elementary school's corn on the cob, Garden Club chili, and a SportsBoosters chocolate banana delight, no nuts. There'll still be tons of choices left for my dinner. I can almost taste it all now.

A terrible thought hits me. *What if I really do have to stay with Andrew and his mother all day?* Not only will I be humiliated, but I might not even get to follow my Fair food plan. I can't bear to think about it, so I have another spoonful of chowder instead.

Penny climbs up on the bench of the next picnic table and walks with her arms out for balance like she's the star of a high-wire act. Lewis follows her with his camera.

I lean my head back and watch thick clouds drift across the dark sky. It looks a little spooky, like the sky in a Halloween story. This reminds me that before Lewis showed up I was thinking about ghosts because of Rip's crazy story. I wonder if those Maynard sisters are really buried in the old graveyard like the old man said.

"And...cut." Lewis turns off his camera and looks around. "Everything's closed, huh? Guess I'm too late for Fair food."

I glance behind me, then side to side. Nothing is happening, and only a few people are still around. Beyond the lights spilling from some of the buildings, tents, and booths, the rest of the town is invisible in the night. I realize I can't even make out the fence at the side of the fairgrounds anymore—the fence that separates the Fair from the graveyard. I'm formulating a plan. My heart speeds up, *thump-thup, thump-thup*, which feels loud enough to make a blip on my sister's radar. I hope it doesn't, because including Painy is *not* part of my plan.

"Your timing is perfect," I tell Lewis, passing him the rest of my chowder.

If we can get Penny to stay with my dad for a while, and if he lets us go off on our own, it'll be the first time I've ever been on the fairgrounds with just Lewis, and no parents. Lewis knows his way around every inch of the fairgrounds—even the places you're not supposed to go—so if there's a way through the fence into the old graveyard, he'll know how to find it. We can check out Rip's story and then explore the rest of the fairgrounds on our own in the dark!

I turn to tell Lewis my idea and find Penny standing in front of me.

"I'm done with dinner," she says.

"Excellent!" I leap to my feet. "Let's go give Dad his egg and cheese."

8
A BEAM OF LIGHT

On our way back to the corn stand, my sister recites a list of every ride she wants to go on. She keeps adding to it, and the rides have to be in a particular order, so she starts over about seventy-three times. I try to get Lewis to hang back a little by digging my elbow into his side. But Penny slows down whenever we slow down, so I never get a chance to tell Lewis my Fair exploration plan.

Dad climbs down from his stepladder as soon as he sees us.

"Hi, Mr. S.," Lewis says.

"Hullo, Lewis. How's life at the movies?"

"A few good shots today."

"Nice!" my dad says.

"Here's your dinner, Daddy." Penny hands him the egg and cheese. "I got you the same thing as me."

"Can we give Lewis a ride home later?" I ask.

"Sure," Dad says. He wipes his hands on the front of his shirt, unwraps his sandwich, and eats half of it in one bite.

Lewis videos my dad and his egg and cheese.

"Mmm-mm-mmm." Dad moves his mouth and jaw up and down and all around like he's acting out "chew" instead of just doing it.

"You still have work to do, right, Dad?" I say.

He shoves the second and final bite into his mouth, moving a little closer to Lewis's camera. "Mmm-mmm," Dad says. He swallows with a loud gulp and turns to me. "Not quite done here, then I have a few odds and ends at your school's eggplant grinder tent." He tips his head toward the blue middle school tent, which backs up to the corn stand. Slinging an extension cord over his shoulder, he climbs back up the stepladder.

"Can Lewis and I walk around a little while you're finishing up?"

"Sure. Be back in half an hour."

Wow! That was easy! I signal Lewis to follow me.

"I'm tired," Penny whines.

"You'll stay with Dad," I tell her. "You can..." I glance around, spotting a mound of hay at the back of the corn stand. "You can make a little bed for yourself." I go over and fluff up the hay. "Here," I say. "Pretend you're a goat or something."

"No," she says.

"Why not?" I argue. "You *like* to pretend stuff."

"Being a goat is dumb. I want to be a kitten." She flops down in the middle of the pile, then crawls around in a circle. "Anyway, this is too scratchy."

The seconds of my half hour are ticking away. I unzip my sweatshirt and spread it on the hay. Penny lies back on it and yawns so wide her tonsils could be characters in Lewis's movie if his camera was on now, which it isn't.

"*Meow*," she says.

"Okay, then." I back away, tugging Lewis by his sleeve.

"Wait!" She sits up and eyes me suspiciously. "What are *you* going to do?"

"We're just going to walk around." I shrug and slow my words down so what I say will sound super boring. And tiring. "We'll walk up the hill...down the hill...around...you know...past all the closed stuff." This is all technically true.

"Okay," Penny says. "*Meooowww*." She pushes onto her hands and knees and turns in circles on the hay.

I let out a long breath.

"Okay," she says again. "I'll go with you. *Meow*."

"You can't!" I blurt. I'm not letting Painy ruin this. "You just said you're tired."

"But I want to—"

"Hey, guys?" Dad calls from his ladder. "I'd like Penny to stay here with me now. Half an hour. Got it?"

"Got it!" I tow Lewis up the hill along the path without looking back.

"What's the rush, Mill?" he asks.

I tell him about Rip and his ghost story. "So I want to go see if there's a hole in the fence, and then check out the rest of the Fair," I finish. "First time on my own, ever! This is so great!"

"Hmm..." Lewis stares off into space. "That guy Rip's story is from, like, ninety years ago..." He flicks one of the camera buttons with his thumb. I can tell he's thinking movie thoughts, and I follow his gaze toward the line of Fair buildings stretching up the hill. The buzzes, trills, and cheeps of insect conversation fill every cubic millimeter of air around us.

"You know what would be great?" Lewis says a minute later. "A shot of you going through the fence. And then a shot of those flying death heads."

I check my watch. "We may not have time to look around the graveyard for them," I point out. "But I definitely want to see if there's a way in, like Rip said. How do we get to the fence from here?"

Lewis glances up and down the path, then ducks into the dark, grassy space between two of the Fair buildings. The sliver of a moon has already set and ragged clouds whoosh past the stars. I try to follow him, but instead I walk directly into a trash barrel.

"Did that hurt?" Lewis asks from behind his camera. "I got it on my infrared setting. It looks all grainy and cool, but I won't use it if it hurt."

"Go ahead and use it," I say, rubbing my ribs.

He waits for me, his camera screen glowing in the dark. It doesn't make a very good flashlight. The grass is long here and it tangles around my sneakers in damp, stringy knots. I hold my hand out in front of me to prevent any more crashes.

A few long seconds later I hit the fairground's chain link fence. It jingles noisily, and the crickets, katydids, and other nighttime callers all stop. When they start up again, they sound even louder than before. On the other side of the fence I can just make out the deep, gray silhouette of a tree here and there across an open field.

"Where's the graveyard?" I ask.

"We're too far downhill. Come on!"

I keep one hand on the fence as we make our way uphill. I've never been behind these Fair buildings, not even in the daytime. I try to picture their fronts but I'm not sure where we are, exactly. Cold air creeps up my back, and tiny droplets of water cling to my eyebrows. I wish I had my sweatshirt.

My watch dial glows in the dark. "We've already been gone seven minutes," I tell Lewis. I peer through the fence into the gloom as we keep going. Soon I start to notice dark shapes on the other side. Some of the shapes are about our height and some are smaller. A few are much bigger. They dot the ground unevenly near the fence and tilt away up the hill at crazy angles like they're about to topple over.

"Mill! It's the graveyard!" Lewis takes off.

I rush after him, feeling with my hand for breaks in the chain link. "I can't find any holes," I call ahead. "Can you?"

When I catch up, Lewis is leaning against the fence in a space between two of the buildings.

"No holes," he says. "It could be a new fence."

"That, or Rip made the whole thing up." I'm mostly sure Rip was kidding when he called me Milton and all that, but I'm not sure about the rest.

"Did you ever hear that Maynard sister story before?" I ask.

"I think my grandma once told me something about an accident in the river. But no ghos—"

We are blinded by a blaze of light. We freeze. High beams sweep across us as a car starts to turn onto the Fair path.

"Take cover!" I yell.

We dive behind the next building. Beyond the fence, crumbling, tilted headstones and their stretched, sliding shadows flash into view and disappear. The night chorus has stopped. The crunch of tires on the path feels loud and near. The arc of the headlights reveals a narrow, black gap between the chain link and a post before the beams swing uphill and the car drives away.

"A hole!" I shout. "There is a hole in the fence!"

9
AN EXTRA DIMENSION

Lewis crouches next to me, aiming his camera at the hole in the fence. The gap in the chain link is a blacker strip of dark about a foot and a half high. From the happy, cheery Fair side of the fence, the murky graveyard side with its tilting headstones looks like a different world. Or a different *dimension*. My brain starts working on this.

"Hey," I put my hand on Lewis's arm.

He jumps. "What?"

"Nothing," I say. "Just, well, remember what I told you from my Theory of Everything project—about the strings and the extra dimensions?"

He lowers the camera. "Not really, but—"

"I told you that for everything to be made of those tiny, vibrating strings, scientists think the universe has to have extra dimensions for the strings to vibrate in. That means not just the three dimensions we know and can see—up and down, side to side, and back and forth—plus time, which is our fourth dimension. Scientists think there might even be *ten* or *eleven* dimensions in all—dimensions with all kinds of weird shapes, even tiny curled-up dimensions. But you can't really picture the extra dimensions. They're just explained with math."

"Mill," Lewis says. "You're the only kid I know who'd think about math at a time like this."

"I'm not thinking about math, I'm thinking about ghosts!"

"Wait." Lewis lowers the camera. "You don't believe in ghosts."

"Well, ever since I heard Rip's story I've been trying to figure out what ghosts could be made of if they *did* exist," I say, talking faster because my idea is so exciting. "So if there are all those dimensions around us that we don't see, then maybe ghosts could exist in those extra dimensions. We'd never even know they were there. It makes total sense! I may have just come up with the perfect tie-in between the Theory of Everything and ghosts!"

Lewis stands up and takes a step back from the fence. "Perfect tie-in as 'Miller's fun idea'? Or perfect tie-in as in 'scientific proof there's ghosts'?"

I grin. "Let's go find out. Flying death heads, here we come!"

"But...but what time is it? Didn't you want to..."

I don't hear the rest because I've already pried the sides of the fence away from the post, and the chingling in my ears as I force myself headfirst into the gap drowns out Lewis's voice. My shoulders are next. Bent ends of the chain link dig into my back like sharp knuckles. I suck in my breath, push at the fence, and pull against the post at the same time. Finally I squeeze through the hole, tumbling onto the ground on the other side.

"I'm in!" I say. "Now you."

"I-I got my fence-hole shot for the movie. I'm good." Lewis glances over his shoulder. "I'll just wait for you here, behind the souvenir booth. I'll be your lookout."

"But you can't shoot the flying death heads from there. We don't even know where they are!"

"Right. So let's come back tomorrow. I'll get better shots in the light."

"What fun is a graveyard in the daytime? Besides, if I have to stay with Andrew's mother, she'll never let us come here!"

"B-but if you really believe that ghosts—" Lewis cuts himself off. "Andrew's mother? What does *she* have to do with anything?"

"I forgot to tell you. I'm supposed to stay with her tomorrow. And Andrew. And Penny. While my mom works at her office and my dad does all of his *and* my mom's volunteer shifts. All day."

He scrunches down again. "You're kidding me," he says.

I wrap my fingers around the heavy chain link. "I wish," I tell him. "What if all I get is this one measly half hour on my own for the whole Fair?" I check my watch. "I mean, this last measly nineteen minutes. This is our chance to see if there's any evidence to back up Rip's story."

Lewis thinks this over. "You're the scientist," he says, shaking his head. Then he shoves the camera through the fence and into my hands.

"Why are you giving me this? I'm not going to—"

"Stay back, ghosts!" he calls. "I'm coming into your dimension!"

As soon as he's through the fence he scrambles to his feet. I hand him his camera and he flips it open. The screen glows.

"Rolling," Lewis whispers.

He grips my arm with his non-camera hand and we pick a path, one step at a time. Even though he knows his way all over town, the graveyard is probably the only place in Holmsbury that Lewis hasn't explored on his own. Not even once. Maybe I shouldn't have told him about my "other dimension" ghost theory. I guess I forgot that Lewis is more superstitious than scientific.

The tall headstones seem to lean in closer as we pass. Worn-down, lumpy ones hide in the uncut grass. All of the night chirpers and cheepers are back at work and the air feels alive. The graveyard may not actually be another dimension, but it feels like it could be.

"D-do you know what a flying death head looks like?" Lewis asks.

"No," I admit.

Something scrabbles in the fallen leaves, then skitters away into the night.

We stumble around, trying to read the dates carved on the stones. Most of them are from the late 1800s, so we move farther away from the fence, searching for older graves. We can hardly see where we're going. Lewis brings

his camera in close to the top of a crooked headstone and we stare at the screen. The camera's infrared light gives us a grainy view of a carved face, round as a full moon, peering sideways at us. It's almost smiling, sort of like the Mona Lisa painting, and it's wearing a crown.

"What are those feathery ear things attached to the head?" Lewis asks.

"I don't know. They look sort of like wings."

"Good. Flying death head. Done." He backs up a step.

"I don't think so. The face looks too peaceful to be called a flying death head. Does the stone even say Maynard?" I guide his camera hand even closer and read from the screen:

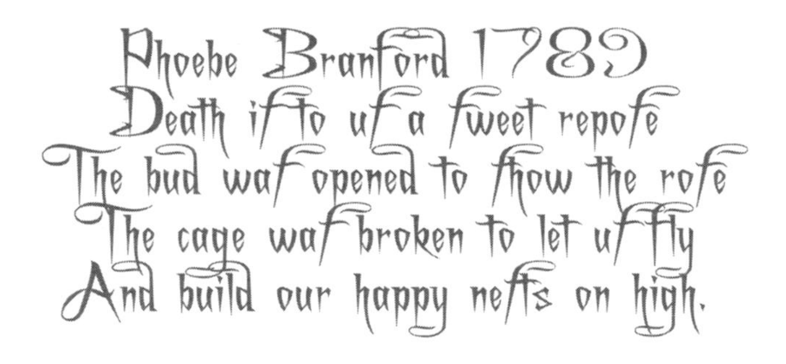

"They were pretty bad spellers," Lewis says. "What's 'fweet' anyway?"

"I don't think that's an f. I think it's an s, like in 'sweet.' 'Death is to us a sweet repose.' Whoever wrote this poem thinks death is a sweet and happy rest in a nest."

"Creepy." Lewis lowers the camera. "Ready to head back?"

"Come *on*." I pull him along. "Let's keep looking."

I stop in front of another headstone. Lewis aims his camera at it and we examine the screen. The face at the top of this stone is not smiling. It's looking right at us, and the wings on each side end in spiky feathers. I try to read the inscription, which is hard since Lewis's camera hand isn't its usual rock-steady self. "'Heve'—no, *here*, I guess—'Here lyeth Micah Biffell.' I mean *Bissell*. 1763,'" I read.

Dearest Micah in his day
Was suddenly seized and sent away
How soon he's ripe
How soon he's rotten
Laid in his grave,
And soon forgotten.

Wind rustles through the trees. Acorns ping against branches on their way to the ground. Lewis ducks.

"'How soon he's rotten?'" he mutters. "This is beyond creepy. Time to get going."

I consult my watch. "We've still got nine minutes to find those Maynard sisters' graves. Just think, you might be the first filmmaker in history to put flying death heads in a movie. You'll thank me when you win an Academy Award."

"Right," Lewis says. He looks over his shoulder toward the fence.

I point to a dark shape tilting into the sky at the top of a hill. "Let's try that one."

It's hard to tell how far away the grave is in the dark. Our climb is steep, and our feet slip in the damp grass. Filmy shapes of trees, shrubs, and headstones stretch away on all sides. When we reach the end of the row, Lewis pans up the height of the pitted stone marker. The R.I.P. 1741 carved in big block print and the glaring skull on top appear extra spooky on the screen.

Lewis's hand is shaking all over the place. "R.I.P." He raises his voice. "Got it!" he calls. "No need for anyone to cross over from their extra dimensions or anything! We're done here!" He turns and marches toward the fence.

"Wait!" I say. "I didn't get a chance to read the name. Did it say Maynard?"

"I don't know and I don't care. R.I.P. means 'Rest in peace,' and that's exactly what I'm letting all of these dead people do." He starts to run.

"Lewis!" I run after him. As I round the corner on a row of stones, my toe catches something. I trip, hitting the ground. *Oof!* Then I'm down in the damp grass, swallowed up by the cricket chorus.

"Mill?" Lewis calls after a minute. "Miller? Where are you?"

My breath's been knocked out of me. I lift my hand to wave, which isn't much help in a pitch-black graveyard.

"Mill!" Lewis cries.

"*Agghh*," I gasp.

He lurches back in my direction.

"Are you okay?" He kneels next to me, holding the lit camera screen near my face.

"Yeah," I manage. I push up on my elbow.

"Look at this," he whispers, pointing the camera at a half-buried nub of stone near my feet. He zooms in.

The Laſt One

We both peer at the video screen.

"The last what?" I ask.

"Who cares?" Lewis aims the camera at my face. "Let's get out of—" His eyes go wide.

"What? Am I bleeding?" I don't remember hitting my head. I pat it with the tips of my fingers.

But Lewis isn't aiming his camera *at* me, he's aiming *past* me. I turn. Behind my head is a smaller gravestone. I scramble to my knees to see what he's looking at on the view screen of his camera.

Carved into the stone's crumbling top is a skull with empty eye sockets and an open, howling mouth. Two jagged wings sprout from either side of its bony cranium.

Eunice M nard, Jan 18, 1738

I drag Lewis toward the next headstone and help him hold the camera sort of still. Another howling skull.

Nabby Maynard, nuary 18, 1738

Then the next stone, with the same awful image.

Rhoda Mayna , Jan ry 1738

"Flying death heads!" I say.

Leaves spiral up from the ground and swirl all around us.

"THE MAYNARD SISTERS ARE COMING TO GET US!" Lewis yells.

We leap up and careen through the graveyard toward the fence.

"Where's the hole?" Lewis shouts. "We're stuck in an extra dimension!" He grabs the fence and shakes it.

"Let's go the other way. Come on!"

We gallop up the hill along the fence and burst out of the graveyard gate at the top. Rounding the corner of the town green like Cooper on a curve, we hurtle back down the hill into the fairgrounds. We don't slow down until we see lights spill across the path from an open door of one of the exhibit barns.

"And…cut," Lewis huffs. He doubles over, pressing his hand into his side.

I start to laugh.

"It's not funny," he insists. But he's laughing, too.

I glance over at the barn doorway and realize we're standing outside the adult baking exhibit, which isn't so funny.

"Speaking of *the last one*," I say, "they probably found that one last piece of my dad's pie by now."

"Well, they took it, right?" Lewis says. "That's good."

"But I don't think they'll judge it since it doesn't follow the rules. I tried to explain everything on this note." I pull the crumpled paper from my pocket. "But I couldn't get it into the dish in time. I bet they already called my dad to tell him he's been disqualified."

Just then, four people step out of adult baking. I pull Lewis toward the corner of the building, away from the lights.

"Whew. Just one category left," a woman says. "Do you really think it's all right if we take a quick break?"

"Sure," a man answers. "It's only for a minute. And we can keep an eye on the door the whole time."

"That's good," another woman says, "because baking judges need to stretch their legs once in a while. *And* get a cup of coffee. It's only one category, but there are a *lot* of pies!"

Pies? I clutch the note in my hand.

Lewis pulls me around the side of the adult baking barn and then to the back. I follow him downhill along the fence. At the lower end of the building he stops and puts his hand on a Dumpster.

"Climb up here," he whispers. "Then push in the swinging door."

"What—?"

"It's the trash chute. Just *go!*"

Without thinking, I hoist myself up onto the Dumpster and feel for the door. When I push on it, light spills out. I push it all the way and peek in. No one is in adult baking.

In three microseconds, I'm in adult baking. Four tables at this end of the building are completely covered with pies. I hurry over and smooth my note out on the first table. Where's our blue dish? I scan the second table. No blue dish there either. Did they throw it out?

"Wait!" I hear a man yell from outside. "I forgot to get cream."

"Hurry up!" a woman calls back.

Just when I'm about to run, I see Dad's entry in the middle of the third table. Trying not to tear the foil, I peel back one edge and slip the note in. I am careful not to touch anything else.

"Okay, let's get this pie show on the road," the man says, right outside.

My heart whumps against my ribs. I race to the wall and dive through the chute.

Lewis hauls me to my feet and we zoom-walk away from adult baking. No one chases after us, which is amazing considering the racket I made barging through the chute.

I remember Rip's words: *They sure liked that note, Myron*, and a smile wells up inside me. I'm sure the judges will like *my* note, too. I can't believe I got it under the foil in time. That was definitely the way to go. My dad *is* the king of pie!

When we're clear of the building, we make ourselves slow down and stroll toward the corn stand.

"Wow! What're the chances we'd be right there when the pie judges left the building?" Lewis exclaims.

"I know," I say. "About four billion to one. Good thing the Maynard sisters scared us out of the graveyard!" Remembering our "escape," I laugh again. "And I can't believe you knew about that chute."

"You find all of the cool stuff when you're at the Fair on your own. You'll see."

"Yeah." I say. Because I *will* see. Tonight is just the beginning. Penny has to stay with Andrew's mother tomorrow but that doesn't mean I have to. Why should it?

My Holmsbury Fair fun meter is going up, up, up.

10
THE BLACK HOLE OF NO FAIR

Somebody is shaking me awake and someone is licking my face, and some of my molecules know that today is the Holmsbury Fair. The rest of my molecules are trying to swim up out of a dream that I'm riding the Gravity Whirl ride with every kid in my class and it spins off of the ground and then way into space so we're whirling around in the Milky Way. Comets shaped like lemons are zooming by and it seems really fun until we spin down, down, down to Earth and land in the graveyard, and then instead of the kids in my class, every rider on the Gravity Whirl is Andrew's mother, or a ghost of Andrew's mother and...

"Miller? Your circuits lighting up yet?"

I open one eye carefully so my eyeball doesn't get washed by Cooper's sloppy tongue. Dad is sitting on the edge of my bed.

"Mom's already left for work. I'm heading over to my first volunteer shift," he says. "You'd better get yourself up and dressed. It's Fair Friday!"

I scratch the Wonderdog behind his flannelly ears while I wait for my brain to come online. *Thwack thwack thwack.* I hear his tail hitting the floor.

"Penny's eating breakfast," Dad says. "Andrew's mother is going to pick you two up soon, so you need to get yourself downstairs to watch for her."

"Yuh." I'm trying to unscramble my thoughts from my dream so I can ask my Dad if I can be on my own at the Fair with Lewis.

"You sure you're awake?" Dad does flying sproings on the end of my bed, bouncing me around. Coop jumps on, too, because he never wants to miss anything fun, and he tramples every part of me, including my head.

"By the way, how'd your sculpture come out?" Dad asks.

I groan. This first-thing-in-the-morning shake-up and head stomping is not helping me figure out how to salvage my Fair Friday.

"Not...a sculpture," I manage.

"Oh," Dad says. "Well, whatever it is, I'm looking forward to checking it out when I get a break." He stands up and heads for the door.

It's now or never, I decide. I sit up and put on my glasses. "Dad," I say, "about the Fair today..."

He stops in the doorway and turns back. "What's up?"

"Well, um, I was hoping...I mean, I really want to..."

I stop and regroup. "I thought I would be on my *own* at the Fair today."

Dad looks surprised. "Hmm," he says in a way that doesn't sound like a flat-out no.

"Not *entirely* on my own," I explain, hoping to increase my odds. "I mean, with Lewis. And not Andrew's mother," I add, just to be clear.

"I hadn't considered you being on your own," Dad says. "And I'm certain that Mom hasn't." He gives me a look that means *and she wouldn't*. He glances at my atomic clock.

"Whoops! I've got to get to my shift. We'll have to talk about this when you check in with me at the Fair. Before the end of my first shift. So before one o'clock. Mom left you a note about it, downstairs. Got it?" He disappears into the hallway.

"Got it!" I throw my covers off and leap out of bed. "Thanks, Dad!"

We'll talk about this later is very hopeful. Maybe even promising.

"Hey," Dad sticks his head back in the door. He looks around as if my sneakers, molecular models, and books are listening, then lowers his voice. "Don't tell anyone, but I can't wait to see how I did in the pie competition."

As he pounds down the steps, he shouts, "I think this year's entry is my best ever!"

I sit back on my bed. Coop tries to dig his nose under my leg and I put my hand on his bony head. Obviously everything's okay with Dad's pie, or someone would have called to tell him it was disqualified. When I get to the Fair, I'll check in on it just to be sure. Then I'll tell him the funny story of how we ate part of it for snack yesterday.

I hear his truck pull out of the driveway. The Wonderdog is staring into my face and lifting one yellow eyebrow, then the other.

"Okay, okay," I say. "I'm coming."

I pull on clothes and stuff my Fair savings—most of what I earned shoveling driveways last winter—into the pocket of my jeans.

On my way downstairs I'm thinking that it won't matter if I have to stay with Andrew's mother for the first part of the day. Lewis and every other kid I know will be at the midway, so I'll get to go on rides with them same as I always do. It's not like I have to go on kiddie rides with Penny and Andrew or anything.

At the kitchen table, Penny is eating a bowl of cereal while she studies the comic on the back of the box. She flicks a glance at me, says "Your shirt's inside out," then returns to the box.

I yank my shirt off and fix it, then look out the front window over the sink. Andrew's mother's car isn't in our driveway. But she should be here any minute because it's nine thirty-two by my watch and the Fair opens at ten.

Even though Holmsbury is a small and mostly quiet town, on Fair days it's packed. There's so much traffic that it takes five times as long as usual to get anywhere, so our three-and-a-half-minute ride will take seventeen and a half minutes. Then we have to park at the high school shuttle lot (four minutes) and take the bus to the gate (five minutes) and then wait in line to buy tickets, which takes even more time.

I let Cooper out into the backyard. That's me being responsible and careful because after we leave he's going to have a long day in the house by himself. Poor Coop doesn't get to go to the Fair at all.

The air in the backyard is cool and the sun is shining

through the tree branches and everything—the orange, yellow, and pink maple leaves, the sharp blue sky, even the dew-speckled grass—looks like it's been colored in with crayons.

"Aren't you going to eat breakfast?" Penny asks me. "I'm having Wheatberry Sunrise Crunch with a banana."

"I'm having a colossal sugar donut at the Fair," I say.

"You can't," she argues. "I ate regular breakfast and you have to eat the same breakfast as me, because Mom said so."

Here's a happy fact: no matter what happens, Andrew's mother will be in charge of Pain-elope today and I won't. "Mom did not say that," I tell her.

"Yes, she did. She left you a note at the table and it says 'eat the same breakfast as Penny.'"

I see a slightly wrinkled note sitting at my place at the table. Since it's from my mom, I'm sure it will have many more instructions than my dad gave me, and I'm equally sure that none of those instructions will be about eating the same breakfast as my sister.

Dear Miller,

Have a great day at the Fair! Andrew's mother will be here to pick you up by the time you and Penny finish breakfast.

I stop reading for a minute to examine the damp smudges next to the words you and Penny and breakfast.

The note smells suspiciously like Wheatberry Sunrise Crunch mixed with milk.

> Please be dressed and ready to go by 9:50. Her cell phone number is 555-6437, just in case. Dad's is 555-1122. Don't forget your Fair money, and please give Penny's Fair money to Andrew's mother. She'll be with you and Penny until six o'clock, when Dad will have a dinner break. At the Fair, please be sure Andrew's mother knows where you are at all times. I don't want her to worry about losing you.

I look at the ceiling. How could any Holmsbury kid possibly get lost at the Fair? We've all been there since we were born and almost every single person working there or visiting there today will be someone we know. I give up trying to think like my mom and finish reading her note.

> I hope to meet you all at seven at the lemonade cart. Dad expects you to check in with him at least ~~twice~~ once per shift.

The cross-out and the word "once" are written in my dad's red pen.

Dad has our blue backpack with water bottles and an extra sweatshirt in it for each of you.
Here is Dad's schedule:

- Firefighter fries booth—10am-1pm
(Dad's shift)
- High school candy apple tent—1pm–4pm
(Mom's shift)
- Elementary school corn stand—4pm–6pm
(Dad's shift)
- Library lemonade cart—7pm–10pm
(Mom's shift)

Please take this note with you to the Fair.

Love love love you,
Mom

PS—Andrew's mother says she'll watch Lewis, too. Isn't that nice?

Oh yes, I think. Lewis will be so thankful. Especially because he's been on his own at the Fair since the third grade and has had years of practice going on rides, looking at animals, and eating Fair food without someone watching him do it.

Penny starts to hum while she chews her cereal. I look up from the note.

"Mom did *not* say I have to eat the same breakfast as you," I tell her. "And anyway, you shouldn't be reading other people's notes."

"Well, I read it because I want a colossal sugar donut," she says, as if that makes perfect sense.

"If you want one, you can buy one with your Fair money. Where is your Fair money, anyway? Mom wants me to give it to Andrew's mother."

"I have it in my pockets. I am going to give it to Andrew's mommy because I am six and *you* aren't that much older."

Today already feels like it's been a week long and nothing has happened yet.

"I'm going up to my room to finish getting my hat ready," Penny says.

I hear a heavy *chlink chlink chlink* as she goes up the steps and realize that her Fair money must be all in quarters—the quarters she's saved from her allowance. I feel sorry for Andrew's mother because she's going to have to lug all that change around at the Fair.

I check the kitchen clock—two minutes to ten—and stare out the window again. I close my eyes and count to twenty, then open them. No car. I walk outside and look across the yards toward Andrew's house. No car. I could have walked from our house to the Fair by now. But maybe Andrew's mother has one of those special parking passes from being on a Fair committee, so she can drive us right to the closest parking lot. We'll still have to wait in line for tickets, though, and walk all the way down to the midway. I decide that I'd better do the responsible thing and call her cell phone, so I turn away from the window to get my mom's note.

"Hi!" Andrew has appeared in the middle of the kitchen, bringing on my usual dose of heart attack.

"Where's your mother?" I ask him.

"Home. She has a headache."

"So?"

I wait. He doesn't say anything because he's staring a hole in the Wheatberry Crunch box. I get him a bowl, pour the cereal, and add some milk.

"So what does that mean, your mother has a headache?"

"It means," he says, taking a break to chew in the middle of his sentence, "that her head hurts a lot inside."

"I *know* what a headache is," I say. "What about getting to the Fair?"

"She wants us to wait."

"But it's after ten already!"

Even if we left immediately, which we're clearly not going to do, we wouldn't set foot on the midway until almost eleven. The all-you-can-ride-for-ten-dollars deal only lasts until four o'clock. I do a quick calculation. That's one dollar and sixty-six cents' worth of rides wasted.

"Wait for how long?" I ask.

Andrew blinks up at me for a few seconds. "Until... her...headache...goes...away," he says, one word at a time, so he's sure I'll keep up.

What if her headache lasts all day? I cross my arms on

the counter and slump forward, face-first. Being stuck here at my house is like being at the edge of a black hole—the black hole of no Fair—where each second takes forever to go by. Meanwhile, over at the Fair, the fun time is ticking away without me and when I get there the Fair will be over.

I hear something clatter, and I look up.

"It didn't break," Andrew says, leaning over the sink where I assume he's just dropped his bowl. He runs out the kitchen door and it closes behind him, leaving me alone with my misery.

11
FAIR ODDS

At ten forty-seven, the phone rings. I wait, like I'm supposed to. After the four rings and the silence while whoever's on the other end waits for the beep, I hear blasting music, about a million voices, and bursts of a happy kind of screaming.

"Mill? You there?"

I snatch up the phone. "Lewis?"

"I'm on my brother's cell phone!" he yells. "Where are you?" His words mix with the clangs and shouts of the midway. The midway! I can't believe he's there and I'm stuck here and the Fair is happening without me.

"Andrew's mother has a headache," I tell him. "She didn't pick us up yet."

"What?" Lewis says.

"Andrew's mother has a headache!"

"What?"

"HEADACHE!" I yell.

"You're not supposed to shout when someone has a headache," Penny informs me from the hall doorway. She is wearing a hat with her Fair ribbons from last year pinned all over it, which makes it look like a shaggy blue, red, and green wig.

"Hold on," I tell Lewis. "Be quiet, Penny. Andrew's mother isn't even—"

"My mom says she'll be ready at eleven fifteen," says Andrew, who's pushed open the front kitchen door. He knocks into a chair on his way in and it teeters on two legs, hangs that way for a time-stopping second or three, then goes all the way over—*crash!* I wonder if it would be considered responsible and careful to lock all the doors the next time Andrew goes out.

"I'll be there soon!" I shout into the phone to Lewis.

I hear "Give me my phone back, elf," then nothing, then the dial tone.

I hang up. Penny takes off her ribbon hat and flops down at the table. Andrew has disappeared again.

"Are you still going to eat a donut?" she asks.

"Yes," I say, though by now I've already eaten two bowls of cereal and an apple since Andrew left. I might not be able to eat a whole colossal sugar donut and still have room for the rest of the Fair food on my plan—the fries, the corn on the cob, the chili, and the chocolate banana delight without nuts, and then dinner. I decide to split the donut with Lewis. If I ever see him.

To keep my mind off all of the Fair things I'm not doing, I take my Fair money out of my pocket and put it in a pile on the table. I count out the five dollars my parents gave me for my Fair ticket and slide it to one side.

Penny stands up, reaches into her pockets, and empties handful after handful of quarters onto the table. This makes a lot of noise. Some of them roll on their edges, so I put my arms across the table in a barrier to keep her money from mixing with mine. Then I sweep all of her quarters back to her side.

"How many dollars did you put in your smaller pile?" she asks.

"I'm not just making any old piles. I'm counting up what I need for different things at the Fair."

She comes over and stares at my five-dollar pile, leaning down closer and closer until her nose practically touches the top bill. I put my hand over it.

"It's five dollars," I say. "Five. For my Fair ticket."

Penny goes back to her chair. "How many quarters does it take to make a dollar?" she asks.

"Four."

She starts making little stacks of four quarters each.

I count out the ten dollars I'll need for my ride bracelet. I add these to my five-dollar pile.

"One, two, three, four, five." Penny taps the top of each stack as she counts. "I've got my money for a Fair ticket, too."

"You don't need a Fair ticket if you're under eleven," I

tell her. "Eleven *is* older than six and that's why it costs me five dollars to get into the Fair."

"Yay. Then I'm luckier than you are."

This conversation is not going my way. I get up from the table and let Coop in from the backyard. He's panting and smiling like he just had the best time and he's sorry I missed it. I refill his water bowl and lock the back door. I want to be ready when Andrew's mother gets here.

"What are those other dollars you put with your five dollars?" Penny asks.

I sigh. "Ten dollars for my ride bracelet."

"Is it free if I'm six?"

"No, it's ten dollars."

While she stacks more quarters I count the rest of my money—even though I already know that I have thirty-two dollars and fifty cents left.

Forty-two dollars and fifty cents is the most money I've ever saved for the Fair. After I buy my ride bracelet, I'm going to play games at the midway and buy a Holmsbury Fair baseball cap and a present for my mom. Her birthday is next Tuesday, and this is the first year I've ever saved up enough to get her something from the Fair. I want to buy her something extra special, since she has to miss most of Fair Friday.

I fold up the dollar bills and put all of my money back into my pocket. It's fourteen minutes past eleven.

"Is it time to go?" Penny jumps out of her seat and starts

shoving quarters into her pockets. They drop on the floor and roll all over the kitchen. We race around trying to pick them up, and Cooper helps by chasing the rolling ones. Suddenly Andrew is back, skidding on the quarters over by the door.

He slides to a stop, barely missing the corner of the table. "My mom said I could stay here for a while," he tells me. He's wearing a yellow duck backpack.

"What?" I sit back on my heels and stare at him in disbelief. "For how long?" I ask.

"You know," he says. "Until we go to the Fair."

"W-we're not going yet?" I sputter.

"Lou-Ann has to stay, too, since she came over already at my house."

The third member of the Pest Pack tromps through the kitchen door wearing shiny pink rain boots. Cooper licks the boots hello.

I get shakily to my feet.

"I have my duck," Andrew explains, "so when we go, I'm ready."

Just then the phone rings. I grab the receiver without waiting.

"Hello?" I say, which comes out more like *Help!*

"Miller? It's...Andrew's mom." Her voice sounds wavery and low. I can hardly hear her. I'm not in great shape at this moment, but I have to admit she sounds a lot worse.

"Miller...so sorry...headache turned into...migraine."

I don't know much about migraines, except that they're not good. "Should we call Lou-Ann's mom?" I ask, because I'm that desperate.

"She's working...in the city...we're meeting at youth exhibit...at six."

"Oh, okay," I say, even though nothing is okay.

"I took medicine...need to rest...if you can hold on just a little longer..."

"Okay," I say again helplessly.

"Thanks, Miller...ohh...better lie down now. Bye." *Click.* Silence. Dial tone.

I hang up.

Penny is poking the rest of her quarters into her bulging pockets. "When are we going?" she asks, without looking up.

"Not yet."

She picks up her hat. "Do we have time for me to tell about all of my last year's ribbons before we go?"

"Maybe," I say. I hope not, I think.

I pace from one room to another through parts of the ribbon recital and the Pest Pack's endless game of Crazy Eights. Andrew's mother still hasn't called. So I call her. No answer. I pace for a few more minutes, then call again. Still no answer.

I make two more circuits around the house and end up back in the kitchen, knowing that I can't wait another millisecond.

"When are we going?" Penny asks.

"Now," I say. "We're going to Andrew's house so his mom can take us to the Fair. She's been resting a long time."

"I'll get my hat," Penny says.

I say "see ya" to Cooper and lock up behind us. That is me being responsible and careful, even though we might just be going three houses up the street and coming back again. When we get to the end of our driveway, Lou-Ann puts the heel of one rain boot against the toe of the other, moving in baby steps. Of course the others have to copy her. Penny can hardly walk with all of the quarters in her pockets. We'd have gotten to Andrew's house faster if we'd crawled there on our hands and knees.

"We have to be really quiet," Andrew whispers. "When I wake my mom before she's ready, her headache doesn't go away."

I make Penny and Lou-Ann wait on the front porch steps while Andrew and I tiptoe into the house. His mom is fast asleep on the living room couch. She's got on one of those eye masks you use to block out the light. I clear my throat. She makes a little whimpering sound and turns over.

Not good, I think.

"How long does she usually need to sleep?" I whisper to Andrew.

He looks at his mother, then at me, and blinks. "Until her head—"

"Never mind," I tell him. "Where's your phone?"

He runs into the kitchen and I follow, reaching out just in time to catch the phone before it clatters onto a glass plate on the counter.

I dial my dad's cell number. It rings and rings and rings, and then I hear, "You've reached Rob Sanford's phone, not Rob. Please leave a message." Which I don't because my dad keeps his phone (a) in his car or (b) in the pocket of a jacket he's not wearing. He never checks for messages until he comes home at night, which my mom says is exasperating. It's definitely not helpful right now. I hold the phone against my forehead and think.

My mom's office is forty-five minutes away. And she's not even in her office because she's out searching for that missing teenager. If I call her in her car she will (a) worry, (b) feel sad that she can't come home, and (c) worry some more. So I hang up the phone and stare at the wall.

I can't believe it's two minutes before noon and I'm in Andrew's kitchen instead of on the midway. That's three dollars and thirty-three cents' worth of ride time gone. Every minute that I'm waiting feels like a year, but my Friday Fair minutes are ticking by faster than nanoseconds.

I hear a thump from the front of the house. Maybe Andrew's mother is awake. I realize that she doesn't expect me to be here, so I sort of say, "Hello?" and head back into the living room. She throws her arm across her face. I see a big book splayed in a heap where it has fallen to the floor. I pick the book up and set it back on the coffee table. One thing's for sure—she is *not* ready to wake up.

An idea begins to spark a few of my brain cells. I got Penny off the bus yesterday, and then I was in charge of Andrew, and then Lou-Ann, too, even though I wasn't supposed to be. And that worked out fine. Well, Lou-Ann *did* get a bloody nose, but she's perfectly fine today. So...since I'm watching them all again now, why don't I watch them *at the Fair?*

I *can't* let them miss this much of Fair Friday. Taking them to the Fair is the responsible thing to do, and I'll be super careful, too. Besides, I'll only be in charge until

Andrew's mother wakes up and meets us at the Fair. Then, if I'm lucky, maybe I'll just be in charge of *me*! All of my brain cells are firing now. I go to the kitchen to find a notepad.

I'm walking the kids to the Fair, I print in big letters.

I pull out my mom's note and copy my dad's booth schedule. I add his cell phone number and write:

Hope you feel better soon. See you at the Fair!

I try to make the bottom of the exclamation point look like a Ferris Wheel, then give up and tuck the note under Andrew's mother's elbow.

I open the front door. "Let's—" I don't finish because I'm talking to myself. I see a mound of Fair ribbons with a brim and a large pile of quarters. I follow a trail of more quarters to the other side of Andrew's car, where Penny is drawing with chalk, and Lou-Ann is skipping around her in circles.

"Where's Andrew?" I ask them.

"In the *treehouse*," Penny says, as if Andrew's location couldn't be more obvious.

When I get Penny's quarters back where they belong and collect Penny, Lou-Ann, and Andrew in one place, I take one look at the three of them and slump down onto Andrew's front steps. The Fair is almost a mile away, there's a lot of traffic, and I've never seen any of these kids stay on the sidewalk for more than three squares in a row. Odds are it'll take us all day just to get to the gate. Maybe this isn't such a good idea.

Running footfalls pound along the sidewalk. I look up.

"Mill, what're you doing?" Lewis's face is flushed and his camera is slung over his shoulder. He's got a blue ride bracelet from the midway on his wrist. "Why are you still here?" he pants. "You're missing the whole Fair!"

"I want to go to the Fair," Penny says.

"Me too," Andrew squeaks.

Lou-Ann stares at me and I have a pretty good idea what she's thinking.

I stand up. "Lewis," I say, "your timing is perfect."

"Uh-oh," he groans. "That's what you said last night, right before we went you-know-where."

"Where?" my sister asks.

"To the Fair!" I say. "We're all walking to the Fair!"

12
AN ALTERNATE UNIVERSE

"In nursery school they tied us together when we went for a walk," Lewis says. He swerves toward the curb for the thirty-seventh time to steer Andrew (or Penny or Lou-Ann) back onto the sidewalk while I try to minimize their detours around trees, bushes, signs, and over other people's feet. Main Street is bumper-to-bumper with cars and lines of school buses that have transformed into parking lot shuttle buses, and they're all traveling toward the Fair at approximately one mile per hour. Which is faster than we're moving most of the time.

"Actually, I think we just held onto the rope," I tell Lewis. His tying-together idea might have made our walk easier today, but we're almost at the Fair now. I can see the lines at the gate.

"We are *not* in nursery school," Penny huffs. "And Andrew has never gone to *any* school, so—" She stops short in the middle of the sidewalk to screw up her face and think, causing a three-Pest pileup. "So he can't even *touch* a rope."

I don't bother to respond to the nonexistent rules of logic on planet Pain-elope. Instead, Lewis and I untangle everyone and guide them toward the herd of people waiting to buy tickets to the Fair.

"This is a good crowd scene," Lewis says, holding up his camera. "I didn't get to shoot anything the whole way here."

"At least we *are* here," I tell him. And to think, it only took four first-grade songs with seventy-three verses each, two skinned knees, and seven heart attacks—Lewis's and mine—after near-flattenings of six-year-olds by Fair shuttles. Also one sore hip where my belt is digging in because Penny's quarters have been weighing my pants down ever since she got tired of carrying them. Which was at the end of Andrew's driveway. It is a perfect Fair day—bright blue sky and not too hot—but I'm already sweating because getting here was a lot of work.

The line for the ticket booths is a six-lane highway of people and strollers. Lewis tries to keep Penny, Andrew, and Lou-Ann moving in just one direction while I count out my five dollars from the no-quarters pocket and put away the other forty-two fifty. Yellow buses with signs that say parking lot names like Douglas Farm, High School, and Fog Hollow Road pull up one after the other, spilling more and more people into the line.

"Hey there, Miller," says my old third-grade teacher, Mr. Jacobs, when I get to the ticket booth window.

"Hi, Mr. J.," I say. But I don't really have time to talk to him, or to any of the other neighbors, friends, and teachers I know in line. I pay for my ticket, then keep my eyes on the Pest Pack while we're being swept along in the sea of Fair-goers. My sister's hat is hard to miss, which is helpful and horrible at the same time.

At the gate, Lewis shows the hand stamp he got when he paid to come into the Fair first thing this morning. I show my ticket and get my hand stamped so I can come back in today without paying again if I leave. Which I don't plan to do.

The hand stamp picture is the Fair mascot, a smiling black-and-white cow, but in purple ink, so my sister and the other two first-graders want their hands stamped even though they don't have to pay to get in. Penny insists on getting a stamp on her other hand and then Andrew and Lou-Ann have to stick their other hands out to be stamped, too. This makes a lot of people behind us crane their necks to see why the line is taking so long and wish they'd picked a different gate.

It's going to be sad when everyone at school talks about what they did at the Fair and all I can say is "I had my hand stamped." But we make it to the other side of the gate, where I hear the music from the midway and smell the kettle corn, and I'm finally feeling the Fair's force field surround me when Penny says, "I'm hungry for cotton candy!"

"Brownie sundae!" Andrew counters.

Penny jumps up and down, making her hat ribbons flap like little flags. "Cotton candy! Cotton candy!"

Talk of food reminds me of my dad's lemon meringue pie, which I'd like to check on before we go find him. I glance at my watch. It's almost one o'clock.

Uh-oh, I think. I yank my mom's note out of my pocket.

"Forget food and rides for now," I tell them. "We've only got eight minutes to meet my dad before the end of his first shift." It would *not* be responsible for me to miss the very first check-in.

"I don't have to meet Dad. *You* do," Penny says. "And I'm really hungry."

In a show of Pest-Pack power, the others line up next to her. Lewis aims his camera at the never-ending throng of people as it divides and closes in again around the obstacle we're making on the Fair path. Heat rises from the pavement.

"Nice hat," yells a voice from the crowd.

Precious seconds tick away. *What was I thinking?* I can't be in charge of these three at the Fair—I can't even get them to walk down the hill! What if Andrew's mother doesn't wake up for hours? And what is my dad going to say about us being here without her?

And then it hits me. My dad won't want me to be in charge. He won't even *let* me. This couldn't have worked out better if I'd planned the whole thing. Except for the migraine part, I guess.

"Listen," I say to Lewis. "All we have to do is get them down to the—"

"I WANT SOMETHING TO EAT!" Penny yells.

I look to see how far it is to the booth where Dad is working. "Firefighter fries," I offer. "Who wants Firefighter fries? My treat!"

"I do," someone I don't know says from farther down the Fair path.

Great, I think.

Lou-Ann bunny-hops over to me in her pink boots.

"Okay, Lou-Ann wants fries," I count her in. "Who else?"

I jab Lewis with my elbow.

"Ow! Right. I want fries!" he says.

"Friarfrighter fies!" Andrew joins in.

I raise my eyebrows at Penny.

She heaves a big, dramatic sigh. "Oh-*kay*," she says. "Fries."

"We have four minutes. Go!" I run toward the Firefighters' booth, holding onto my pants so Penny's quarters don't pull them down.

"Mill!" Lewis yells.

I spin around in time to see Penny, Andrew, and Lou-Ann disappearing in different directions as if they have just blown apart in the Big Bang. Not one of them is following me. They already look smaller. In another second they'll be tiny particles lost in the roiling frenzy of the Fair universe.

"STOP!" I bellow.

ried

A surprisingly large number of people on the Fair path stand still. And all of them stare at me.

"Impressive," Lewis says.

"Why is Miller Sanford yelling at everybody?"

A girl is pointing at me. I recognize her from Room 24, the sixth-grade class next door to ours. But I can't worry about her now.

Lou-Ann is farthest away from me, because she's the fastest. For the moment she's not moving, and neither is Penny. Andrew is closest to me because he tripped and is picking himself up. Although losing the three of them in the mob of Fair-goers could solve many of my problems, it would probably cause many more. So I imagine myself in a parallel universe where no one knows me or will ever see me again and I yell, "COME BACK NOW!"

And they do. This is so surprising that for a few seconds I think I actually *am* in a parallel universe. The crowd oozes down the Fair path around us.

"What?" Penny demands, as if I'm annoying *her*. "You said we were going to Firefighter fries."

I check my watch. Two minutes to one. A bunch of high school kids carrying band instruments swarms us and for an instant I lose sight of my sister, Lewis, and the others. I stick my hand through a gap between a girl and a tuba and grab onto Penny, because now I'm truly desperate.

"Hold hands and don't let go," I order, hoping no one will notice or, even worse, take our picture for the *Holmsbury Times*.

Andrew holds onto Penny's other hand and Lou-Ann clomps into line behind him.

"Go!" Lewis calls from the back. "Full speed ahead!"

He raises his camera and we whip down the hill like a vibrating string decorated with Fair ribbons, a yellow duck backpack, and pink boots—a string that clanks eighty-four pounds of quarters as it goes.

13
CHARGES

We make it to the Firefighter fries booth with twelve seconds to spare. Even the air tastes like fries. The line stretches past the apple crisp booth, beyond the whole length of the Farm Museum, and then it keeps growing as more people join in alongside the museum's field of antique tractors. We're not far from the midway, so we're being blasted by Fair sounds. The music, the yelling, and the bells, whistles, and popping noises of the games all blend together in one super-loud, happy mash-up.

I pull my string of six-year-olds around to the booth's back doorway and let go. Only about a thousand people saw me drag them down the hill, but it will all be worth it now that my dad can take charge. I am so relieved to see him standing next to the bubbling oil vats that my throat feels suddenly thick, and I wonder for a second if I'll start my day at the Fair by crying right here next to Firefighter fries.

Then Andrew trips into Penny, who topples past me through the doorway, toward the fryer.

"Whoops," Dad says, catching her. "Hot stuff in here." He pulls off his grease-soaked apron and herds us away from the door.

"Hullo, all," he says. "Nice job on the hat, Penelope. Very fancy." He holds his watch up and gives me a pointed look. "Cutting it close..."

I take a deep breath. "I know, Dad, I—"

"We came here for fries," Penny interrupts.

"In a minute," I tell her, even though the line will probably be more of an "in an hour" kind of thing. "Dad, I—"

Dad ducks back into the booth and comes out with a giant paper plate heaped with fries. They're still sizzling.

"Freebies," he says. "These came out all stuck together. Careful, they're hot."

Penny grabs the plate and flumps down on the grass. The other two land next to her and they attack the fries like a school of piranhas. Lewis captures it on camera.

Good. I don't have to spend any of my money on fries, and we don't have to waste any of the ride time we have left waiting in this line. Things are looking up.

"Okay, have fun," Dad says. "I've got to sprint up to the candy apple tent for my next shift."

"Dad, wait. We—"

He's backing away, up the hill. "Don't worry, I remember what you asked me. We'll make a plan with Andrew's mother at the next check-in. But try not to come right at the end of the shift." He looks behind me, and around the area. "Where is Andrew's mother?"

"That's what I'm trying to tell you!" I say. "She's not here."

"She's in her house with a migraine headache," Lewis fills in.

"What?" Dad says. "So she just dropped you guys off?"

"Well, no. We sort of walked," I tell him.

"*Just you two with these three?*"

"Andrew's mother took medicine and fell asleep. I left her a note, Dad. I tried to call you."

"Call? Uh-oh." Dad steps back inside the fries booth and comes out with our blue backpack in one hand and his jacket in the other. He fishes his phone out of a jacket pocket. "Six missed calls," he reads from the phone. "Andrew's mother, you, and four from Mom." He looks up quickly. "Did you call her?"

"Um…no," I admit. "I thought she would worry a lot."

"Oh, yes," Dad says, "she would worry a lot."

"I walk here all the time, Mr. S." Lewis says.

"True." Dad looks up the hill, then back at us. "And you've been on your own at the Fair before, haven't you, Lewis?" he asks.

My heart surges.

"Since third grade," Lewis reassures my dad.

Lewis is not looking my way, on purpose. And I am not launching up in the air like a balloon rocket. On purpose.

"Good," Dad says. "So you two know to be careful? To stay together?"

"Of course we'll stay together," I assure him. "That's the whole idea."

Dad motions toward the French fry feeding frenzy. "Don't let them out of your sight," he warns.

Them?

"But Dad—I can't do that! It was so hard to get them here. I thought *you* were going to take over now!"

"Me?" he says. "I've got all of these shifts to work." He looks at the little kids and shakes his head. "I know you wanted to come to the Fair, Miller, but maybe it wasn't such a good idea to—" He stops. "Hang on," he says.

He leans in the back door of the fries booth. "Anyone want to cover a shift at the candy apple tent?"

"See the line out there, Rob? You should just stay *here!*" a voice shouts from inside.

"I know!" I say, grabbing at an idea. "Maybe you could ask someone up at the candy apple tent to stay on for *that* shift."

"Hmm," Dad says.

This "hmm" is the opposite of a promising "hmm." My hopes sink through my sneakers into earth core territory. My dad is good at lots and lots of things, but I'm remembering now that chatting up parents he doesn't know so he can ask for a huge favor isn't one of them.

"Okay, here's what we'll do," he says, "at least until Andrew's mother gets here. Instead of once every *shift*, I want you to check in with me *hourly*. So your next check-in will be at two o'clock. You cannot be late. You took on a big responsibility today, Miller, and I know you can do it. I've got to head up the hill, but the rest of you should go get your ride bracelets and start having fun."

"Rides!" Penny shouts, springing up from the grass.

"Bracelets!" Andrew chimes in.

Lou-Ann waves the empty paper plate in the air, which probably means that she wants to go on rides, too. It also means I didn't get any Firefighter fries.

"Miller and Lewis are in charge," Dad tells the first-graders. "Stay with them at all times. Understand, Penelope?"

"Oh-*kay*," she says.

"Got it, Andrew and Lou-Ann?"

"Yes!" Andrew smacks himself in the forehead in some sort of salute.

Lou-Ann sidesteps her pink boots next to my sneakers.

"Miller," Dad continues, "you know where I am. We have a two o'clock check-in. But you can also call me from the pay phones next to the midway." He puts his phone in his pants pocket and pats it. "You have change?"

I nod miserably. He hands me a couple of quarters anyway, and I add them with a *tlink* to the eighty-four pounds of quarters already in my pocket.

"Two o'clock check-in," Dad says. He takes off up the hill, then makes a U-turn and comes back.

"Let me know if you go into adult baking," he says. "A buddy of mine swung by here and said something I didn't catch about my pie. He was smiling and laughing so it must be good news!" Dad grins, then disappears into the crowd.

His slice of lemon meringue pie got judged after all, and it must be on display at the Fair. That's good news.

But then there's the bad news: I'm still in charge of Painy and her Pest Pack.

14
SPACE, TIME, AND FAIR PROBABILITIES

The music and shouts of the midway exert a magnetic pull, so I don't have to hold any Pest Pack hands to steer them in the right direction. But every square millimeter of space that isn't filled with a ride or a game booth or a food stand is thick with Fair-goers who keep getting in our way and breaking up our traveling blob. And even though someone shouts "Hi, Miller!" every few seconds, I don't ever look to see who it is because I'm too busy keeping my eye on my sister's ribbon hat and counting off *one, two, three*—Penny, Andrew, Lou-Ann—over and over.

Lewis stops. "Stand there." He swings his camera to direct us toward a spot under the Ferris Wheel. "Move over a little," he tells us. "Right there. When the cars come around it'll look like you're getting kicked in the head."

"Which kind of pie did Dad enter, anyway?" Penny asks

me while we wait for Lewis to frame his shot. "Lemon meringue, like yesterday?"

In my sister's universe, it's perfectly reasonable for our dad to have been at the Fair all day and night yesterday doing electrical work *and* to have baked another pie at home at the same time.

"Exactly like yesterday," I say.

Legs dangle from the pink, mint green, and blue Ferris Wheel cars swooping up and over our heads. We all crane our necks and lean back to watch the cars rise into the air. *Rides!* Even being in charge of three little kids can't spoil the fun of rides.

The sun is on my face and the music is pounding in my ears and I'm standing there soaking up that midway feeling when Andrew tips all the way over backwards and clonks into my knees.

"Good one," Lewis says from behind his camera.

I pick Andrew up by his duck, dust him off, and set him on his feet facing the ticket booth.

"Take out your ten dollars," I tell him. I raise my voice so Penny and Lou-Ann can hear me over the seven billion decibels of midway noise. "Line up at the booth for your ride bracelets."

Lou-Ann stands at my elbow while I pull a fistful of quarters out of my pocket and hand them to my sister. Penny squats down and counts four of the quarters into a pile on the ground. Then she counts out a second pile. A boy races through the line, kicking the quarters.

"Hey!" Penny grabs up her money.

I give her more quarters. "Just count it all at once," I say. "Count to forty."

"No. I'm doing groups," Penny says. "Ten groups of four."

"You're going to end up with zero groups of four and no ride bracelet if you keep spreading your Fair money on the ground."

Lewis slings his camera over his shoulder and holds out the hem of his T-shirt. "Dump 'em in here," he says. "I'll give her four at a time."

Lou-Ann watches me drop handfuls of my sister's quarters into Lewis's shirt. Then she watches as I take out my snow-shoveling money. I think through the numbers. Even though we've missed more than half of the ride time, it's still worth it to buy the bracelet. I can ride thirty rides between now and four o'clock, and paying for thirty rides separately would add up to a lot more than ten dollars.

I count out ten dollars and put the thirty-two fifty I have left back in my pocket. This seems like a lot of money, but I'll need all of it if I want to play games, plus buy treats, a baseball cap, and the special birthday surprise for my mom.

Lewis steps up to the booth with Penny and starts giving her stacks of four quarters. She pushes each stack through the window. "ONE...TWO...THREE..." She finally makes it up to ten. Lewis gives me back six extra quarters, and I drop them into my pocket with the leftover ton that's still pulling my pants down.

"My ride bracelet is the special kind with blue on the outside and white on the inside." Penny shows off her wrist, as if hers isn't the exact same ride bracelet every kid on the midway is wearing.

Andrew shrugs out of his duck pack and fishes around in it. He produces a sweater, two good-sized rocks, a ruler, and a purple plastic shower cap. Finally he pulls out a zippered pencil case, repacks the rest, and totters over to the line.

I hear the woman in the ticket booth tell Andrew, "Put your wrist out. No, hold still. Just wait—hold it—oh, never mind! Next!"

"Look!" Andrew waves his arm around. "I got the fancy kind!" He shows us his ride bracelet, which is blue and white on the outside, and blue and white on the inside, because it's twisted like a Holmsbury Fair version of those never-ending Möbius strips in my mom's book of drawings by this super-mathematical artist named M. C. Escher.

I step up to buy my bracelet. Lou-Ann is right there next to me, staring at the ten dollars in my hand. She doesn't get in line. *Uh-oh*, I think.

"You don't have ten dollars, do you," I say.

Lou-Ann doesn't say anything, of course. She looks even smaller than usual, like a scared little rabbit.

• Ferris W
• Cow Lif
• Animal P
• Bitty B

"My mom has Lou-Ann's Fair money," Andrew informs me.

That would have been helpful to know three hours ago. I still have lots of Penny's quarters in my pocket, but probably not another forty. Slogging everyone up the hill again to find my dad would waste even more time, so I decide to use ten of my extra dollars. My dad will give me the money back later.

"It's okay," I tell Lou-Ann. "I've got ten dollars for you. Put your wrist up to the window."

She skips over to the ticket booth. I count out an extra ten dollars and stuff my remaining twenty-two dollars and fifty cents back into my pocket. I hand twenty dollars through the slot at the bottom of the window, and Lou-Ann and I get our bracelets with blue on the outside and white on the inside. She flashes me a smile, then runs over to join Penny and Andrew who are watching a clown on stilts twist long, skinny balloons into hats and poodles.

"Finally," I tell Lewis. "Let's go on a ride!"

"I've done all the good ones at least once, Mill," he says. "You pick."

"Deal!" I turn to survey my choices and notice a wooden sign painted with planets and shooting stars. A tall, stick-thin man is standing near the sign.

"Hey, there's Rip," I tell Lewis. "The old guy I met in adult baking—you know—the one who told me the ghost story."

"Where?"

"This way." I grab Lewis's shoulders to point him in the right direction. "The guy with the white hair, and the red and black—"

"Never mind him," Lewis says, under his breath. "Look at *her*."

A woman in flowy skirts with a bright purple head scarf is watching us. Underneath the planets and stars on the sign are spooky red letters that read: "POSTRENIKA PREDICTS!! $2!!"

"You!" The woman crooks her finger at me.

"What do you think she wants?" Lewis mutters, hardly moving his lips.

"Postrenika will make a prediction for you," she calls. "First part *free*!"

Out of the corner of my eye I see Lewis slowly aim his camera in her direction. A knot of people gathers.

"No recording!" The fortune-teller points a long, black fingernail at Lewis. "You interfere with my portal to the spirit world!"

"And c-cut." He lowers the camera.

She closes her eyes and raises her hands into the air. "Contact me, spirits!" she commands.

People stare. Lewis sucks in a breath. Why did I have to see Rip here, of all places, and point him out right now? I consider space, time, and Fair probabilities while we waste more ride minutes waiting for the spirits to speak.

"I sense something," she says. "A message. Yes!" She

opens her eyes and swirls toward the crowd. "*Someone is missing!*" She swirls back to me. "There. You want to know more?" she says. "Two dollars!"

I give my head a quick shake. No thanks.

"I've got two dollars!" A high school girl waves money in the air. "Tell me something about *me*!"

Postrenika looks at me for another second. "Next!" she says, taking the high school girl's money.

"*Someone is missing*," Lewis repeats. "And she looked right at you. Weird."

What's weird is that someone *is* actually missing—the girl from my mom's work. But my mom has explained lots of times about confidentiality, so I don't mention that coincidence to Lewis.

He snaps, pointing his finger in the air. "You know who's missing?" he says. "The youngest Maynard sister."

"From Rip's story? Why would *my* prediction have *her* in it?"

"Maybe you're connected." Lewis's voice shifts into science fiction movie mode. "*Across the dimensions*."

"My toe *did* connect with a gravestone last night," I snicker. "Maybe it was hers."

"Let's look." He flips open his camera and we examine the shaky image from the night before.

"Huh," I say. "There's no date and no name. Just 'The Last One.'"

Lewis stares at the screen. "Didn't that guy Rip say the

three Maynard sisters'll haunt the cemetery until they find their missing sister?"

"Come *on*. Don't tell me you really believe that story."

"Maybe they haven't found her yet." Lewis's eyes widen. "What kind of grave has no name and no date? An *empty* one, that's what!"

"But—"

"And how about this?" he adds. "R-I-P. Rest in peace. Get it?"

"No-o-o," I say, because I don't. At all.

"Rip!" Lewis repeats. "Rip is the perfect name for a ghost!"

"Whose ghost?" I give him a skeptical look. "The Maynard sisters were *women*. Rip is a *man*."

"Not one of the sisters. *The carriage driver*."

I'd forgotten about that part of the story. "Well, Rip's alive, not dead. But if there really was a carriage driver, there should be a man's headstone in the graveyard with the same date of death as the Maynard sisters," I say, thinking out loud. "We could go back to the graveyard and check for one sometime."

"No way!" Lewis reacts as if I suggested we eat live cobras. "You want to go back into that graveyard? Count me out!"

A riot of screams reach us from the BlastoCoaster.

"What are we doing?" I exclaim. "Come on, guys, rides!" I turn toward the balloon-twisting clown. He's gone.

So are Penny, Andrew, and Lou-Ann. In their place are about two thousand strangers.

"Where are they?" I look from spot to spot in rising panic. "They're gone!"

Whap! I am walloped over the head by a balloon giraffe.

"We want to do rides and you're supposed to take us!"

15
MOLECULES OF HOPE

We've got half an hour to do rides, then we have to check in with my dad at the candy apple tent," I tell Lewis and the first-graders.

"So, where to first?" Lewis aims his camera at the huge grin spreading across my face, then pans in a slow circle.

We're on the midway at the Holmsbury Fair, I've got a blue paper bracelet on my wrist, and every ride is waiting. There's something fantastically fun in every direction—the Mile-High Flying Swings, the Pirate Ship rocking in its huge arc, the crazy Spinning Teacups. Off to the right I see a domed disc lifting up off the ground. It starts to turn in a slow circle, then picks up speed.

"The Gravity Whirl!" I shout.

"Great," Lewis says. "Let's go."

"We're not going on the Gravity Whirl," Penny says, tossing her popped giraffe into a trash barrel for emphasis.

"We're not tall enough for the Gravity Whirl," Andrew points out.

My grin falls away. "But—"

"Hey, Miller!" Henry Yee, a boy from our class, runs up to me with his sister Susannah, who's in the fifth grade. "We're going on the Gravity Whirl. Come with us!" Henry is bouncing on his toes like he's about to launch into space.

Susannah looks behind her. "Bye, Mom!" She waves.

"Mom?" A molecule of hope forms in my mind. "You're here with your mother?" I search the crowds and hone in on Mrs. Yee. She's wearing a bright orange shirt and a cheery smile. More molecules of hope expand into a long chain of hope. Mrs. Yee waves at me. I wave back. Excessively. Because I'm having a brainstorm of brilliance.

"There she is!" I say.

Henry's mother was my sister's kindergarten teacher last year. Penny loves her, every other kid in the school loves her, and Andrew will love her even though he's homeschooled and has never seen her before. Mrs. Yee is the best grown-up I could have hoped for to help me out. She's with a roomful of kindergartners every day, so three first-graders will be like a vacation to her. My dad will think this is such a great idea that I don't even have to ask him first. I grab Lewis's arm.

Henry is inching toward the Gravity Whirl. "We're helping Mom with our little cousins," he says.

Little cousins? I let go of Lewis.

"There's five of them here with us," Susannah adds. She pushes Henry along like they're in a hurry. "They're in nursery school so they can't go on any of the good stuff. Mom said we could ride the Gravity Whirl while they go on the Bouncy Slide."

I feel like I've been unplugged. My shoulders droop. I take a closer look at Mrs. Yee. There are two little kids holding her hand on one side and three on the other.

"HI, MRS. YEE!" Penny yells. "I'M GOING ON THE BOUNCY SLIDE, TOO!"

"First the Mini-Swings," Andrew says.

"FIRST THE MINI-SWINGS!" my sister yells.

Lou-Ann points to the Gravity Whirl and shakes her head no.

"WE CAN'T GO ON THE GRAV—"

"Okay," I say, stepping in between the human megaphone and Mrs. Yee. "She gets it."

I get it, too. Mrs. Yee would have been the best, most perfect grown-up to take charge of the Pest Pack, but she can't do it because she has a Pest Pack of her own.

The other information slowly seeping into my brain cells is that six-year-olds can't ride the Gravity Whirl. They can't ride the Zipperator. They're not going on the Pirate Ship, the Rockin' Rounder, or the SuperDrop. Six-year-olds are not tall enough for the real rides at the Holmsbury Fair. Most of my molecules of hope float away into space. I drag my gaze toward the kiddie end of the midway and catch one last glimpse of her bright orange shirt just before Mrs. Yee disappears into the moving throng of Fair-goers.

"Have fun on the—" I turn back to Henry and Susannah, but they're already gone.

I swallow. *I'm* the one who decided to bring these kids here without Andrew's mother. Not Lewis. He shouldn't suffer because of my stupid idea.

"Go ahead," I tell him. "Go with Henry and Susannah. You don't have to stay with me. Really."

"Nah." He shrugs. "It'll be a good chance to get some other kinds of shots for my movie. Besides," he adds, "Andrew's mom might even get here by the next check-in."

"She might," I say. Out of the corner of my eye I see the Gravity Whirl spin and spin.

16
MOVING OBJECTS

After a large amount of dodging and weaving and a medium amount of six-year-olds smashing into each other and into other people, we make it to the kiddie midway. Penny, Andrew, and Lou-Ann line up at the entrance to the Mini-Swings. Lots of their friends from school are in line, too. Lewis and I are the only eleven-and-a-half-year-olds anywhere near this ride. We lean against the metal barrier with the rest of the ride-watchers—all grown-ups.

When Penny gets to the front, she shoves her bracelet wrist right up in the ticket-taker's face. The guy looks right past her as if almost getting punched in the nose is just another of the many boring parts of his job.

The swings are bucket seats on long chains, with a safety bar to keep the kids in. Andrew starts to clamber onto one, falls out, and tries again. My sister tosses her ribbon hat at me, then runs around the circle inspecting each empty swing. I hold the hat low at my side and hope no one thinks it's mine.

Seated in a swing, Lou-Ann pushes her safety bar up and down and looks at me.

"I'll hook it for you," Penny yells from her swing on the other side. "I'm six, and Miller isn't much more than—"

"Stay in your swing," the ride guy says. "I'm coming around to clip all of you in."

I turn my back to the Mini-Swings so the handful of people on the fairgrounds who missed the announcement might think Penny was talking about someone else. I watch the regular rides on the other side of the midway swoop, turn, and spin. I close my eyes, listen to the screams, and pretend I'm on the SuperDrop.

"Hi, Miller! Hi, Lewis!"

Three kids from our school run past us in a blur. One of them is holding a gigantic bag of kettle corn. I don't have kettle corn on my list, but seeing it reminds me that the only item I've had from my Fair food plan so far today is a whiff of Firefighter fries. My stomach grumbles.

"The swings slowing down makes a great close-up shot," Lewis says.

I turn around and see the swings wind down from their maximum speed—turtle—to their medium speed—slug. They barely moved fast enough to get any centrifugal force going. After a few minutes the Mini-Swings slow down so much that they're almost not moving at all. Andrew struggles with his safety bar.

"Hey, Andrew!" I call. "Wait until it stops."

He looks up. He doesn't seem to be able to undo the clip.

Good, I think.

Then I see him try to slip out without unclipping, which he might be able to do because he's so bony. He gets partway out, then gets his foot stuck.

Bad, I think.

"Don't move!" The ticket guy sprints around the circle of swings.

I vault over the barrier and race toward Andrew, gripping my belt to hold up the quarters. With one leg free and one caught in the swing, he tips over so he's hanging upside down. He's holding on to the safety bar with his hands, and his hair is brushing the ground. When we get to him, the ticket guy unclips the bar and I grab Andrew under his arms.

"I'm okay," he squeaks as I haul him upright back into the seat. "Perfectly okay."

"Geez, kid," the ticket guy says, breathing hard. "Stay put on the rides until the operator lets you out!"

I set Andrew on his feet and straighten the straps of his duck backpack. His hair is decorated with wisps of dry grass and some dirt.

"Does your head hurt anywhere?" I ask.

"Nope," he says. "I didn't hit my head at all."

Pcorn

I check anyway. No blood. No bruises. I bend his right arm, then his left.

"Let's see you shake your legs," I say.

All of his parts seem to be working as well as they usually do, so I walk him away from the swings.

"Okay?" Lewis asks.

I nod.

He holds up his camera and his thumb. "Classic!"

Penny and Lou-Ann stumble to the gate as if they've spent the last five minutes traveling to the moon at warp speed. The ticket-taker goes back to the boring parts of his job. My heart rate slows from quadruple-time to double-time.

"Where's my hat?" Penny demands.

I spot the pile of bright ribbons on the ground next to the barrier.

"I'm not trusting *you* with it anymore." She stomps over to pick it up.

There's a bonus, I think.

"Hey, Penny!" a little girl yells from the line in front of the Mini-Swings. "We got a blue ribbon for our class pear butter!"

"Yay!" my sister shouts. Then she turns to me. "I want to see my new ribbons. Let's go to the youth exhibit!"

I glance at my watch. "Not now," I tell her. "It's already time to head up to the candy apple booth to meet Dad."

"Goody!" she says, ditching the ribbon idea. "You didn't treat us to fries, so you can buy us candy apples instead."

"What are you talking about?" I say. "You got fries."

"We didn't get fries from *you*. We got fries from *Dad*."

"Fries are fries," I say, knowing that's probably not true on planet Pain-elope.

Here on planet Earth, I'm hoping that my dad will do the buying of the candy apples. I'm also counting on him to give me back my ten dollars for Lou-Ann's ride bracelet. And I still have one large molecule of hope that some grown-up will take charge of the Pest Pack so I can be on my own. But that will never happen if we miss our next check-in.

I survey the jam-packed midway. "We're on time, and we're still going to be late!"

"Follow me." Lewis leads us around the back of the Mini-Swings and we squeeze, one by one, through a gap between two sections of metal gate. We head uphill, scrambling over wires and hoses, and duck between two trailers.

"These're the midway workers' places," Lewis tells me.

"I never even knew they spent the night here," I say.

We keep going uphill. Lewis waves us around a wooden storm fence and we come out next to a bunch of hot tubs.

"Where are we?" I ask Lewis. "Did we leave the fair-grounds?"

"Nah," he says. "This is the Home and Garden part of the Fair."

He might as well have said that this is the Andromeda Galaxy part of the Fair, since I've never seen any of this. I stretch my mind around this new information as we tromp through a display of wooden yard sheds.

Penny, Andrew, and Lou-Ann start playing tag around the sheds. Every time one of them disappears behind a little building I get a jolt of panic.

"I really need a break from worrying about the location of these three moving objects," I tell Lewis.

"Here's an idea." He opens a shed door.

Penny materializes. "You can't go in there," she tells him.

"I've been in these sheds a hundred times," Lewis says.

My sister hops into the shed and the other two scramble after her. Lewis shuts the door. We lean our backs against it. Giggles and thumps come from inside.

"Excellent," I say to Lewis. "Thanks."

Outside the shed the sun is shining and the midway music floats up from down the hill. I feel the Fair's force field tugging at me. I close my eyes and take a long, deep breath—the smell of new wood flavored with a whiff of fried dough. I imagine myself in a parallel universe where the first-graders play in this shed long enough for me to go on the Gravity Whirl with Lewis, or see the weird chickens, or do something—*anything*—on my own at the Holmsbury Fair.

"LET US OUT!" Penny yells.

17
A WARP IN THE SPACE-TIME CONTINUUM

I spot my dad as soon as we get to the candy apple booth. His back is to us, and there's a wide patch of sweat in the middle of his T-shirt. He's got on a heavy apron and oven mitts, and he's stirring a gigantic copper kettle of steaming red goo.

"Hey, Dad," I say. "We're all here, just like you wanted. And it's"—I check my watch—"two minutes before two. Pretty good, huh?"

"Yes, good," Dad says. He doesn't turn around.

"Hi, Daddy!" Penny yells.

"Hi, Mr. S.," Lewis says.

We crowd in for a closer look. The air around the tent smells thick and sweet.

"Stay back," a woman warns us. She's wearing an apron, too, and a white chef's hat with a crown drawn onto it with markers. The Queen of Candy Apples, I think. "Get ready for the first fresh batch of the shift," she yells toward the back. "Trays up!"

Inside the tent, grown-ups are washing apples, shoving sticks into apples, tossing the stuck apples into barrels, and filling rolling racks with huge, flat trays in a top-speed candy-apple assembly line. Lewis captures the action. I recognize the high-school chorus teacher from our all-town concerts, but I don't know if the rest of the workers are parents or teachers or what, because I don't go to the high school yet.

"Lew-Lew!"

Lewis's brother is at the front of the tent, selling candy apples. Two other high school kids are working with him. They hand out apples and take in money, hand out apples and take in money. Business is booming.

"Ned!" Lewis grins. "*Score!*" he says under his breath. He disappears behind the tent.

I wait for Dad to look over at us, but he doesn't.

"Running low!" one of the girls at the front yells.

"Hit it, Rob!" says the queen of candy apples. She yanks a tray off the rack. "Remember, dip quick."

Dad grabs an apple from the barrel next to him. He holds it by the stick and dunks it into the kettle.

"Not too deep. Watch your hands. Give it a twirl, then put it here." She holds out the tray, lined with wax paper.

The first candy apple my dad sets down on the tray looks a little lopsided.

"Dad, did Andrew's mother call?" I ask.

"Not yet. I can't talk now, Miller," he says over his shoulder. "Everybody doing okay?"

I step sideways to block his view of Andrew, who still has a few pieces of grass in his hair. "Yes," I say.

"Good work. See you here at three."

"But—"

"Next apple," the queen orders. "Dip, twirl, set." She checks a thermometer clipped to the side of the kettle. I see that she's got Band-Aids on her fingers and a bandage on her arm. "Give it a stir every once in a while, Rob," she tells Dad. "We don't want the sauce to burn."

I don't want my dad to burn, so I don't ask him for candy apples. Or for Lou-Ann's money. And it's pretty clear that there hasn't been a warp in the space-time continuum that allowed him to find a grown-up to take over being in charge of the Pest Pack, so I don't ask him about that, either. Since my mom's the one with friends at the high school, I'm reasonably sure that my dad hasn't said much of anything to anybody here at candy apples. Even parents who are big talkers wouldn't ask people they've just met to take care of their little kids.

While the others watch the apple assembly line, I check my mom's note. My dad's next shift doesn't start until four o'clock at the Holmsbury Elementary School corn stand. He knows *lots* of people at the corn stand.

Good, I think.

But that's two long, annoying hours from now, and ride bracelet time ends at four.

Bad, I think.

I hear loud jingling and look up. Everyone on the Fair path moves aside. A team of gigantic horses clops by pulling a cart, their hooves echoing on the pavement. Across from me, on the other side of the path, I glimpse a red and black checked shirt. I spot Lewis near the back of the tent and motion for him to come over.

"What?" he asks.

"Look over there. Quick, before the horses get in the way. It's Rip."

"Which one is he?"

"The really tall one—with the white hair. Near the picnic tables." I point with my elbow so it's not too obvious. "That way."

Lewis flips open his camera. "I'll pan the crowd and you can pick him out for me after."

"Hurry up. He'll be hidden behind the first horse in a few seconds."

"I'm on it."

The horses continue down the hill, and people pour onto the path again. I lose sight of the red and black shirt.

Lewis turns the camera off. "We can check this in a minute," he says. "Hey, Penny! Look what I got!" He runs around the back of the tent again and returns with two candy apples on a paper plate.

"YAY!" Penny and Andrew yell.

Lou-Ann claps her hands.

Lewis offers them one of the apples. "You guys share this."

They huddle around it and we move into the shade to eat ours.

"I knew Ned would have a stash of rejects," Lewis tells me. "I have to wash the dishes for him for a week. But it's worth it."

He takes a bite, then passes the apple to me. The coating is caved in on one side. The fruit is crisp and the red candy is hard and crackly, and so sticky it glues my teeth together. Candy apples aren't my favorite, but at this point I'll eat any kind of Fair food I can get.

"Now for Rip," Lewis says. He wipes his hands and flips his screen open.

I watch closely as the camera moves over the crowd in replay. Rip isn't there. "You didn't get him," I say.

"I got everyone," Lewis is staring at the screen. "I aimed right where you pointed." He raises his head slowly. "Mill, he's not there *because ghosts don't show up on video!*"

"You've seen one too many scary movies," I say.

"No," he insists. "That's true about ghosts. Everybody knows that!"

I hand the candy apple back. Lewis just used the same exact words that Rip used about the Maynards: "everybody knows that!"

"Well," I say, shaking off the shiver of cold air that slipped along the back of my neck, "this is only one piece of data. You've got to repeat the experiment and get the same results. Try to get him on video again."

"Okay. But you'll see I'm right," he says. "It's a true fact."

I stare at the ground, mulling over my ghost matter theories. If ghost matter is made of neutrinos, it probably couldn't send light waves to the camera's sensors. And what if ghost matter is really subatomic strings that exist in some other dimension? Could that appear on video?

Pink rain boots appear on the ground in front of me. I look up. Lou-Ann is standing next to Lewis, staring at what's left of our candy apple.

"What?" he says to her.

She looks from our apple to the apple core Penny is holding, and back again.

Lewis sighs. He hands her the rest of ours.

"For a kid who doesn't talk, she sure has a lot to say," he observes.

"Miller!" Dad calls.

I hurry over to him.

"I'll have a break at three," he says without looking up from apple dipping. "Penny and her pals can hang with me then."

"Hang with you?" A giant bubble of happy rises in my throat, and I work hard to make words come out around it. "And...and...and...I can...go...with Lewis?"

"Watch it, Rob!" The queen of candy apples shouts. "You're boiling!"

Dad jumps back as splinks of hot red candy sauce erupt from the kettle. "Yup." He grabs the stirring spoon and fights back.

It wasn't a mistake to bring them to the Fair after all. It's actually paying off! I leap over to Lewis and shake him by the shoulders. With one eye on my sister, I tell him our news. We low-five, behind our backs. Three o'clock!

Over in Pest-Pack land, Penny and Lou-Ann have gooey

red faces. Andrew has his own candy coating. Both candy apples are gone. Even the sticks look like they've been chewed. But who cares about candy apples? There'll still be an hour of ride bracelet time left after three o'clock. I can cram twenty rides into that hour if I plan it right.

Painy's internal radar registers a blip. "What are you smiling about?" she asks.

"Rides," I say. "Rides are fun. Let's go back to the midway!"

18
GHOST THEORY

We take Lewis's shortcut in reverse, minus the stop at the garden sheds. I'm being extra responsible, doubly careful, and quadruple-super-nice to Painy and her pest pals. It's hard work, but I only have to hang on for forty-nine more minutes.

I picture every ride I'm going on, in order: Gravity Whirl, Pirate Ship, BlastoCoaster, Zipperator. I stop to let the others go ahead of me out of the Home and Garden area, through the wooden storm fence toward the kiddie midway. Penny goes first, then Andrew, then Lewis.

"Wait," I say. "Wasn't Lou-Ann with you?"

"I thought she was up with you," Lewis says.

I make one complete revolution. No pink rain boots in sight. "Lou-Ann!" I yell. Of course, there is no answer. "The rest of you, stay right here!"

I charge back in the direction of the hot tubs because that's where I saw her last. But she could be anywhere in this moving obstacle course of people. Lou-Ann is tiny. She's only six. And if I call her she won't answer. My stomach twists as tight as a ball of rubber bands.

"LOU-ANN!" I yell. I run through the maze of hot tubs.

Her head pops up between two giant spas. My knees bend like spaghetti so I hang onto the side of the tub nearest me for a second. Lou-Ann raises one of her pink rain boots and tips it upside down, pouring a waterfall of gravel and dirt onto the ground. She disappears between the spas again.

"Wait!" I thread through the hot tubs and find her sitting and tugging on her boot over bare toes.

I hold out my hand. "Don't *do* that!" I tell her, pulling her to her feet. "You can't just stop somewhere. We thought you were lost!"

Lou-Ann gets that rabbity look again.

"Oh, hey—it's okay," I say quickly. I pull in a deep breath. "Just let me know next time you need to stop."

I walk her back to the storm fence, hanging onto her hand until we meet the others and reach the kiddie midway again.

"Hard to keep track of," Lewis observes.

"I don't know if I can do this much longer," I say as we walk over to the entrance for the Bouncy Slide.

The slide attendant repeats, "shoes-off-get-in-line, shoes-off-get-in-line" over and over as if she's an animatronic Fair attraction. The little kids kick out of their shoes and run into the snaky line, which moves up the slide's steps and separates into three chutes. After they go up the steps I hear my sister bossing everyone around at the top so she and Andrew and Lou-Ann can slide down at the same time, three across. They scream all the way from the top to the bottom. Well, except for Lou-Ann, whose mouth forms a silent O visible above the small and somewhat gray soles of her bare feet.

"She'd make a great silent movie," Lewis says from behind his camera. "All I need is some of that fast, tinky piano music for the background."

Andrew trips his way out of the Bouncy Slide exit wearing his own left sneaker and somebody else's five-sizes-too-big right sneaker, so Lewis takes him back to make a sneaker trade. After that, they all climb right into the next ride, the Loco Choo-Choo, without having to wait. The train is not the slightest bit loco and it barely choo-choos, which explains why there's no line.

I check my watch. Only two thirty-five. Part of Albert Einstein's Theory of Relativity shows that moving through space is connected to moving through time, so the slower a clock moves through space, the faster it ticks. But I'm not moving and I'm surrounded by extra-slow-motion kiddie rides and the minutes on my watch aren't ticking by at all. What would Albert have to say about that?

At the other end of the midway, I see the Pirate Ship rock

way up to one side of its long arc. The Ferris Wheel circles around and around. I check my watch again. A few minutes have ticked by, but three o'clock is still twenty-four minutes away. Penny, Andrew, and Lou-Ann tumble out of the Loco Choo-Choo. Lou-Ann scampers off.

"Wait!" I run after her.

She pulls up in front of the Bitty Bumper Cars and all three six-year-olds plow into the long line. The line surges ahead, then stops while the next set of "drivers" spin around in circles and honk for three endless minutes.

While they're waiting in line, Lewis flips open his camera. "Did anyone else talk to him last night?" he asks, looking at the screen.

"Talk to who?" I look over his shoulder at the video of the cart horses. "Oh, you mean Rip?"

I run through what I remember from the adult baking building. Mr. Hansen from the hardware store must have talked to Rip. No, no he didn't. I try to picture the other grown-ups on the committee—the ones who were carrying all of the cakes and pies to the back.

"Rip was sitting on the bench with me. He talked a lot. But I don't remember him talking to anyone else."

"Think about it, Mill," Lewis says. "He appears three different places, you're the only one who sees him, then—*poof*—he's gone."

"Well, he didn't disappear from adult baking," I point out. "I was the one who left."

But while I watch Penny and the others climb into the bumper cars, I'm remembering that Rip did just sort of show up there. And he basically vanished when Mr. Hansen took the bar off the door, then appeared again when I was heading out of the building.

"If I go with your theory that Rip's a ghost," I tell Lewis, "and that's a big hypothetical *if*, then why do I see him at all? Why me?"

The bumper cars start up. Andrew wedges his royal blue car into a corner, front end first. Lewis aims his camera at the car.

"Maybe ghosts can tell that you know all that 'other dimension' stuff," Lewis says. "The fortune-teller picked you out, too, remember? Or maybe..." He looks up from the camera for a second. "Maybe Rip wanted you to go to the graveyard."

"So I could trip over headstones?" I joke.

"Laugh if you want, but I bet it's something to do with those Maynard sisters," Lewis says. "Maybe he's helping them find *The Last One*."

"Oh, and that's me? I'm their youngest *sister*?"

"I don't know," Lewis says. "I mean, well, no."

"We don't even know how much of that old story is true," I remind him. "Finding the carriage driver's grave would help."

Electric buzzes and crackles erupt from the tops of the bumper car rods. We watch Penny's car bash into Andrew's

9
4
8

and get stuck. Then Lou-Ann crashes into them in a three-car stall. They honk their horns and turn their steering wheels in place until the ride ends.

"And...cut," Lewis says.

He runs the scene backwards, then shows me the bumper car crunch-up at double speed. It's comic genius.

"Look, Mill," he says. "If I were you, I'd stay away from the graveyard. I wouldn't even go behind the souvenir booth and look through the fence. I, for one, am done with flying death heads!"

"*I'll* go on the Flying Death Heads with you," Penny says, out of nowhere.

"It's not a ride," I tell her. "And besides, this isn't your conversation."

"But Lewis said it's behind the souvenir booth and I want to—"

"Never mind what Lewis said. *Dad* said to be at the candy apple tent at three o'clock." I check my watch for the trillionth time. "It's seven minutes to three. We have to go. Grab hands!"

We haul them through Lewis's shortcut and up the hill at a jog. *Chlink chlonk chlunk* go Penny's quarters in my pocket.

Dad is at the back of the tent, pushing sticks into plain apples. Lewis gets a shot of the overflowing barrels of freshly wrapped candy-coated ones all around the inside of the tent. Ned is gone, and three new high-schoolers are doing the selling.

"Get your candy apples!" one of them calls.

The candy apple queen nods at us. "Rob, we're way ahead now. Take your break."

He unties his apron and comes out through the back of the tent.

"Still no word from Andrew's mother," Dad says. "You're doing a great job with a big responsibility, Miller." He puts his hand on my shoulder. "You've earned some time off to have fun on your own."

He motions us onto the grass to let someone in a wheelchair pass.

"How come Miller gets to go by himself?" Penny complains. "I'm almost as old as he is."

And how old will she have to be to stop saying that? In my mind, I click off the Pain-elope channel.

"Race you to the Gravity Whirl," I challenge Lewis. The entire Fair stretches away down the hill in front of me. Now it feels like my hill. My Fair. I crouch in sprint position. "Ready?"

Lewis slings his camera over his shoulder. "Cut between the SportsBoosters and the roasted peanuts booth," he directs, "then around the picnic tables, past the center stage, and straight across the field."

"Set..." I lean forward.

"Go!"

"Be back at three twenty, boys," Dad calls.

My brain says stop, but momentum and a pocketful of

quarters pull me a few steps farther down the hill before my feet cooperate.

"Only twenty minutes?" Lewis mouths at me.

I hitch up my pants and race back to Dad. "I thought...I mean...can't we—"

"Attention Fair-goers," an announcer says over the loudspeaker. *"Come see the artists at work in the first ever Holmsbury Fair giant pumpkin carving contest. The judges are about to select the finalists!"* A few notes of trumpet music follow.

"I *knew* there was giant pumpkin carving." Penny aims her giant told-you-so face at me.

"I knew, too," Andrew pipes in. "My mom told me. Can we go?"

"Sure," Dad says. "Miller, you guys are going to have an even longer break at six. A whole hour on your own. Is this Fair turning out great for you, or what?"

"Great," I say. I'm trying to mean it, but ride-bracelet time will be long over at six. I shove my hands in my pockets and hit quarters. "Dad, could you at least keep Penny's Fair money?"

"Sure," he says. He puts his hand out and I start to empty my pockets.

"Whoa." Dad makes a bowl with both of his hands. "No need to carry all this around. They can use change for the candy apple money box. I'll trade it in."

"Thanks," I say.

I take a springy, lighter step and remind myself that

twenty minutes are better than zero minutes, which is the amount of fun I've had at the Fair so far. I'll just have to pack an impressive number of rides into twenty minutes.

"READYSETGO!" Lewis yells.

We take off down the hill.

19
A LEMON MERINGUE METEORITE

Lewis and I blast onto the main part of the midway, neck and neck in the stretch. We run flat out until we hit the metal barrier for the Gravity Whirl.

"Tie!" I yell.

We jog around the barrier, looking for the end of the line. Lots of kids I know from school, and plenty I don't, are waiting to ride.

"Hey, Miller! Hey, Lewis!" Henry waves at us. "Time off from watching the little guys?" He raises his fists in the air. "Us, too."

His sister, Susannah, points in front of her and makes a space. She and Henry are only about twenty kids back from the Gravity Whirl's entry gate. Behind them the line stretches all the way to the edge of the midway.

I look at the space Susannah is holding for us. I'm figuring that most of the kids in line have probably been on every ride two or three times by now. I've waited all day for this chance. When I get my next break, the ride-bracelet time will be up, so this could be considered a ride *emergency*. Lewis and I exchange a guilty glance.

"Don't even think about it," the big kid behind Henry warns us.

I shrug at Susannah. "Thanks, anyway."

"It's worth the wait," she calls, as we wind toward the back of the line. "This is our third time on it!"

We keep going, past the Pirate Ship, past the Zipperator, and then past the BlastoCoaster. Lewis turns his camera off when we finally find our place behind the five hundred and seventy-two other kids already waiting.

"Maybe the line'll move super fast," Lewis offers.

We see the Gravity Whirl rise way up into the air. It starts to spin slowly. A group of kids pulls into line behind us.

"I don't know if I can go again," one of them groans, cradling his stomach. The skin around his lips is the green-gray color of lunchroom string beans.

"I'm glad I didn't eat much yet," I tell Lewis.

"I got a great shot of barf this morning, anyway," he says. "Want to see?"

"That's okay," I say. I watch the Gravity Whirl pick up speed. "Did you video the Gravity Whirl from underneath?"

I know from experience that if you stand under the Gravity Whirl and look up you can see the riders appear and disappear in nanosecond-long flashes. They're pressed against the inside walls with their faces flattened from centrifugal force like laundry in the spin cycle.

"Good idea!" Lewis says. "Hold my place!" He darts off toward the ride's entry gate.

The Gravity Whirl is spinning at top speed now. I look around at the other rides and shift from foot to foot. I peer past the kids ahead of me. The line hasn't moved at all. I roll onto my toes trying to see over the shoulder of an eighth-grader who lives on my street. She turns around and says, "D'you mind?"

I try to look somewhere else. A bright orange balloon escapes into the sky and I watch it sail over the top of the Ferris Wheel. Away across the fairgrounds, rivers of people flow in every direction. A clang from the Hammer Striker pulls me back to the midway and I spot a red and black checked shirt near the entrance.

"It's Rip!" I turn to Lewis. But he isn't here to collect ghost data, because he's off shooting the Gravity Whirl like I told him to.

Rip is standing under a big oak tree at the corner of the Farm Museum. Since people are walking *around* the old guy and not *through* him, this probably means he's not the ghost of some long-dead, made-up carriage driver who's trying to help the ghosts of three long-dead sis—

My brain stops in mid-think as a woman emerges from the shade behind Rip. Rip tilts his head and says something in her ear, pointing up the hill. She nods. Shaking out her apron, she gathers the long skirts of her old-fashioned dress and sweeps away to the right along the path. I see Rip walk uphill.

Without thinking, I take a step out of line.

"Mill!" Lewis is all the way up the line on the other side of the BlastoCoaster, heading toward me. "Don't you want to ride?"

I take my eyes off of Rip just long enough to flick a worried glance at the lengthening tail of the Gravity Whirl line.

"I can hold your place," the kid behind me says, "if you're coming right back."

"Thanks!" I tell him. "Lewis—turn on your camera and follow me!"

I charge around moving and stationary bodies on the midway, trying to keep Rip in sight.

"Where are you going?" Lewis calls.

"It's Rip!" I shout over my shoulder. I look uphill again. The distance between me and the moving patch of red and black is growing. My progress slows to a frustrating crawl, with no way around or through the near-solid matrix of people clogging the path. At an intersection of three paths, I stop.

"Where is he?" Lewis huffs. He raises the camera.

I shift onto my toes to search. "I don't know which way he went."

Lewis stares past me, tapping his camera. "He appears only to you...he tells you about a lost Maynard sister...and that Postrenika tells you about someone who's lost, too. It's all gotta mean something."

Two girls from seventh grade stroll by, sharing skinny-sliced onion rings from a paper cone. I catch a whiff of the greasy, crunchy goodness and my stomach wrings itself inside out.

"I don't know what all that 'lost' stuff means, but I know what *this* means." I point to my watch. "Only four minutes left! It's too late to go back to the Gravity Whirl now. I must be the only person in Holmsbury history to spend two and a half hours at the Fair, go on zero rides, and starve!"

A sweet, cinnamony scent wafts by.

"Then how about a colossal sugar donut?" Lewis motions at the cart behind me with his camera. There's only one customer waiting.

"Excellent!" I say.

Lewis shoots a close-up of Mr. Fortescue, who owns Holmsbury Grocery, as he slips one of the amazing, dinner plate–sized donuts into a bag for the kid in front of us. The kid whisks the bag away from the swarm of yellow jackets hovering above the sugar-sprinkled counter.

"Should we split one?" I ask Lewis.

"Sure," he says. "They're huge." He shuts off his camera and digs into his pocket.

"No, I'll buy it. You got the candy apples."

"Yeah, but with future dishwashing," he points out.

"That still counts."

The kid holds his bag in his teeth while he takes out his money.

"Too bad the Gravity Whirl line was so long," Lewis says.

I check my watch again. "We'd better get the first-graders first, *then* eat the donut," I tell him.

"They're going to want some," he warns.

I consider what happened with the Firefighter fries and the candy apples.

"Two, please, Mr. Fortescue," I say.

"That'll be nine dollars, Miller." The grocer puts two gigantic, beautiful donuts into a bag.

When I count out nine dollars for the donuts, I've only got thirteen-fifty left. *Thirteen-fifty?* I do some quick Fair math. I paid at the gate with my mom's five dollars, but then I spent ten dollars of my own forty-two dollars and fifty cents on a ride bracelet, so that left thirty-two fifty. After taking away nine dollars for the two donuts, I should have twenty-three dollars and fifty cents. But I'm ten dollars short. *Lou-Ann's ride bracelet!* I didn't ask my dad for the money back yet. But I'd better. Thirteen-fifty won't get me very far at the Fair.

Lewis and I each pinch a hunk off of the top donut. "I'll get to go on a ride when we take the little kids back down to the midway," I tell him, "even if it's not one of the super-fast ones. And speaking of fast"—I stare up the hill, chewing—"I can't believe I lost sight of Rip again like that. For an old guy, he sure can move."

"You didn't lose him," Lewis says. "He *disappeared*. That counts as evidence."

DONU

We hear a loud *beep-beep* and jump out of the way as the Fair path clears so the soda truck can get through. My dad's friend Harry is driving.

"Hey, Miller!" he shouts. "Ask your dad if he's working on an invisible apple pie for next year—ha ha ha!"

What? A speck of worry pokes at my brain. I meant to tell my dad about eating his pie, but I haven't had a chance to check on it yet. I hope everything's okay.

Harry lets out another big laugh, then drives on. *Beep-beep!*

"Invisible apple pie?" Lewis scrunches his eyebrows together.

"How could I forget?" Mr. Fortescue slaps the side of his leg and laughs. "That note and your dad's pie—hilarious!"

I open my mouth, then close it. *Hilarious?* My speck of worry expands to the size of a large lemon meringue meteorite. My dad told me one of his friends was laughing about his pie. Then Harry. Now Mr. Fortescue.

Everything is definitely *not* okay. They're all making fun of my dad's entry.

The grocer is waiting for me to say something. "Uh, yuh," I manage.

How does Mr. Fortescue know about my note? *What have I done?*

I turn, smash into Lewis, and propel him along the path by trying to walk through him.

"I'm doomed!" I moan. "Why did I write that note? Why did I try to enter one crummy slice of pie? I should have just told my dad we ate it. Now I made everything a megamillion times worse!"

"It wasn't a crummy slice of pie, Mill," Lewis says. "It was the best ever. Your dad's the king of pie."

"That's right." I pull up just short of the candy apple tent. "And now I've turned the king of pie into the biggest joke of the Holmsbury Fair!"

20
THE LAWS OF PROBABILITY

As soon as Lewis and I get to the candy apple tent, I shake the white paper donut bag like I do with Cooper's biscuit box at home. It works just the same way—it draws the Pest Pack like a magnet. They stick to me, and I hurry them down the path. I don't hang around to ask my dad if he can give me Lou-Ann's money back or if I'm getting another break or if he's enjoying everyone else's great big laugh at his one slice of pie.

"See you at the corn stand at four o'clo—" My dad's words are swallowed by the distance I've already put between us.

I don't want to be around to hear anyone else make fun of his pie. And if I don't come up with a way to make things right before he finds out about the big "joke," I can probably forget about having any more time off at the Fair for the rest of my life.

But schools in other towns are starting to let out and about a hundred thousand more people are at the Fair, so it takes every molecule of my brain power to keep track of the three first-graders. When I stop at the bottom of the hill, Penny lunges at my hand, and I grab the top donut just before the bag holding the other one disappears in a swirl of grubby six-year-old fingers. Two milliseconds later the bag is shredded and their donut is gone. They turn their attention toward ours, so Lewis and I stuff the rest of it into our mouths. Choking down a colossal sugar donut with a side helping of lemon meringue panic was not part of my Fair food plan.

"We went to the giant pumpkin carving with Daddy," my sister informs me. "And we got chocolate milk. What did you do?"

"We came down here to do rides." I swallow my last dry lump of donut.

"Which ones did you go on?" Andrew asks.

I sigh. "None."

"That's dumb," Penny says.

I have to agree with her. But not out loud.

A group of kids barrels into us and our unstable electron, Lou-Ann, splits off from our cluster. I catch sight of her pink boots and grab for her thin shoulder through a tangle of other bodies.

"Too many people were at the giant pumpkin patch," Andrew says. "I couldn't get inside to see any of the jack-o'-lanterns."

"Me neither," Penny says. "And I wanted to go the whole way inside."

"Look," I tell them. "It's three-thirty. Ride bracelets are over at four and I haven't been on a single ride yet. For the next half hour we have to do rides we can *all* go on."

"The Happy Coaster!" my sister yells.

It would be impossible to invent a more babyish ride. "Absolutely not," I say.

"The Ferris Wheel?" Andrew asks.

Lewis shakes his head no. "Longest line at the Fair."

Lou-Ann points at the House of Mirrors. The line looks okay. Last year my entire class went into the House of Mirrors together, and the ride attendant let us have a really long turn. We laughed the whole time.

"That could be fun," I say.

But as soon as we go in, Penny has to provide everyone in the House of Mirrors with an infinite number of reflections of her Fair ribbon hat. Next, Andrew disappears. So I leave the others with Lewis and scour every mirror for his yellow duck pack. Shapes stretch and undulate alongside me while kids collide with me, the mirrors, and each other. I hear Penny "helping" by yelling directions to everyone, including strangers. A blotch of yellow flashes by.

"Andrew!"

I follow his shape-shifting blob through the maze until I see the doorway to the end, with the grass and the rest of the Fair beyond. Andrew pops out of a side hallway, giving

me my fortieth helping of heart attack for the day. He clunks, forehead first, into the last mirror.

"I'm o-kay," he says. "Perfectly o-kay."

Lewis, Penny, and Lou-Ann are already outside.

"Great stuff!" Lewis taps his camera. "What's next?"

This is hopeless. I'm about to give up on rides altogether when the full, happy sound of a waltz drifts by. The carousel! Why didn't I think of that before? We always ride it together—Penny, Mom, Dad, and me. It's goofy, but kind of nice, too. "Follow the organ music!" I say.

We get there in time for the next turn. Lewis and I strap Penny, Lou-Ann, and Andrew onto their horses, then start looking around for our own horses. As the carousel begins to turn I'm thinking about my dad's pie, and before I realize it I wind through the horses until I'm just about back where I started.

"Mill—where were you?" Lewis twists around in his saddle. "I tried to save you a horse."

There's no empty horse near Lewis now, so I circle the platform again. I end up on an inside horse next to Lou-Ann's. At least I'm not sitting on a bench with all the grandparents. I'm going up and down and catching a Fair breeze, so it's still a little bit fun. But I can't see much, so my brain still has lots of free space for pie worry.

As soon as we climb off, Andrew leans over and throws up fries, candy apple, chocolate milk, and donut. Beating the laws of probability, he manages a clean shot, missing his clothes and shoes.

"I'm not hungry anymore," Andrew says, in case we were wondering.

"Let's get you a drink of water," I tell him.

Everyone takes turns at the fountain.

"Are ride bracelets over?" Andrew asks, wiping his mouth with the back of his hand.

I check my watch. "In twelve minutes they are."

"One more ride! One more ride!" Penny chants.

Lou-Ann grabs my sister's hand and they jump around, which brings them in contact with at least seven other people. I make seven apologies.

"Okay, one more ride," I say, hoping it doesn't cause more jumping and bumping. "One with a *short* line. You up for it, Andrew?"

He hiccups. "I'm up," he says.

He seems like his usual self, so I steer them between and around the seventeen billion people muddling up every square nanometer of space. At the edge of the kiddie midway, Lou-Ann breaks our hand-holding string and runs to the Jungle Tree House.

"Go ahead." I say, letting go of the other two.

Penny and Andrew scramble to join Lou-Ann at the end of the line. When Andrew finally succeeds in climbing through the rope tunnel into the Tree House, I turn to look back at the rest of the midway. The Zipperator is spinning, the Teacups are whirling, and the High-Flyer Swings rise into orbit with riders's legs dangling in the air. Ride-bracelet time is over, and all I did was walk through the House of

Mirrors—which technically isn't even a ride—and go around on the carousel. I yank off my paper bracelet and throw it in a trash barrel.

"That stinks, Mill," Lewis says.

"I know." I jam my hands into my pockets and lean against the metal barrier.

Lewis pans across the midway, ending at the vampires, werewolves, and veiny eyeballs painted on the front of the Tunnel of Terror.

"I used to skip this whole side of the kiddie midway because of the Tunnel of Terror," he says.

"We've still never been in it."

The black iron gate hangs off its hinges. Wailing, groans, and evil laughter spill out from deep inside.

"And it still looks like about as much fun as a flying death head," Lewis says. "Which reminds me"—he lowers his voice—"you're not still thinking about going back to the graveyard sometime, are you?"

"I'm done with that. All I'm thinking about now is a way to fix my dad's pie reputation."

"I don't get how your note could've made things worse." Lewis flips his camera screen open and closed. "What's wrong with those judges, anyway?"

"Maybe notes aren't allowed," I say. "Or maybe I made a dumb mistake on it because I wrote it so fast."

"What are you going to do?" Lewis asks.

"The only thing I can do. I have to go up there and

explain everything in person," I say, deciding. "The judges need to know that I didn't mean for my dad's pie to be a joke, and that it is really the best lemon meringue pie ever baked for the Fair, then eaten up by mista—"

"Who ate up Dad's Fair pie?"

We both bolt up into the stratosphere. Lewis comes back to Earth first.

"The judges," he tells Penny. "They taste all the pies."

"But they don't eat them up!" she points out at forty billion decibels, in case people on Neptune don't know that.

"Not usually," I say.

And though the judges don't usually change their minds, I've got to make that happen, too. Without Painy there to mess things up.

How am I going to manage *that*?

21
NEGATIVE MOMENTUM

"I SEE MY TEACHER AT CORN ON THE COB!" Penny yells. She lets go of my hand and dives through the family in front of us to get to the corn stand. I keep my eyes trained on Andrew and Lou-Ann as they break away and follow her.

I wonder what my dad will say about us being ten minutes late. On our way here from the midway we couldn't get to Lewis's shortcut, and half the time we were trying to go up the hill it seemed like we were moving backwards. Negative momentum—moving in the wrong direction. We had so much negative momentum I'm amazed we made it to the corn stand at all. During ride-bracelet time the Fair is always full of kids and parents from Holmsbury, but everybody in the state of Connecticut must be here by now.

"Fun hat, Penny! Hello, everybody!" Mr. Caffrey says. He

brushes butter on an ear of corn and hands the paper boat across the counter to a customer. "People love Holmsbury Elementary corn, but I wish we could serve it faster." He points his butter brush at the line snaking toward the town green. "Good thing your dad's here having a look at our broken butter melter." He smiles across at the customers. "Who's next?"

"I'll help you, Mr. Caffrey," my sister says.

"I'm going to find my dad," I tell Lewis.

I edge past a four-foot-tall ear of corn with feet. It yells, "GET YOUR FREE CORN!" and holds out a paper boat full of samples. People crowd in. Everyone wants a taste because Holmsbury Elementary corn is world famous.

"Turn this way," Lewis directs the corn.

While I head back toward the cooking area, I hastily devise a two-pronged emergency strategy for this four o'clock check-in. Part one: get in and get out in microseconds so there's no time for my dad or anyone else to talk about pie. Part two: keep Pain-elope away from my dad so she can't tell him what she overheard me say about his pie being eaten up.

I spot him digging through a toolbox. The electrical insides of a butter melter are spread out on a cloth next to him. Tall trees at the back cast lengthening shadows across the people shucking corn on the other side of the kitchen. Steam billows skyward from the two corn boilers.

Free corn!

"Hi, Dad," I say, staying outside the cooking area fence, since inside it's adults-only. "Sorry we're late—it's really crowded."

"Miller! How's it going? Everybody doing okay?" He takes a small silver something out of the box and leans over his work.

"Yup," I say, keeping it short.

"Mom called," he says.

Uh-oh. Did he mention to my mom, the president of worriers, that I had the genius idea to walk Penny, Lou-Ann, and Andrew all the way to the Fair? And that now *I'm* in charge until six o'clock, just with Lewis, and no grown-ups? I really can't imagine that conversation.

Of course, I'm heading for a much worse conversation with my dad about pies, notes, and Fair jokes if I don't get to adult baking before he does. He's been waiting all day to find out how his pie did, ribbon-wise. I'm sure he'll head right over there when he gets his break at six. I'd better have something to say to him about his pie before then, and I'm hoping it will be something good.

Right now Dad is too busy to talk, and Penny's up front helping her teacher. Both parts of my four o'clock check-in strategy are working.

I look past the corn-shuckers in time to see my own teacher pulling aside the back flap of the middle school's eggplant grinder tent. Bags and bags of the long grinder rolls are stacked along the inside. Mom says these eggplant grinders are her favorite sandwich in the world.

"Hi, Ms. Valencia," I call to my teacher. She waves, then ducks into the tent.

Dad is still concentrating on his repair job.

Good, I think.

"Okay, then," I say. "See you at five, Dad." I whip around to leave and slam right into my sister.

"Andrew threw up at the carousel," she announces.

I guess I should have filled Lewis in on my check-in strategy. Especially part two—keep Painy away from my dad.

"Andrew is sick?" Dad looks up.

"Really sick," she says. "There were chunks of—"

"He's fine," I cut her off. "Fair food plus rides. You know." I use the oldest, wisest, and most casual tone of voice I can muster. "He threw up. He feels better. Everything's good." I try to shoo Penny along. "You have work to do, Dad, so we'll see you later."

"If you're sure," Dad says.

"I'm sure."

Dad looks at his watch. "It's almost four thirty already, so let's make the next check-in at five thirty. I'll be done fixing this butter warmer by then, so I think I can give you and Lewis another break. Only a short one, though."

A break? That means I can head straight to adult baking at five thirty and fix everything. *Without* Penny!

"Daddy," Penny says. "Miller said—"

"Who wants to put on the corn costume?" Mr. Caffrey calls out. "We need a new volunteer to hand out samples."

"I do!" Penny scoots off toward the front of the stand.

Saved! I say a hurried good-bye to Dad and follow her. When I get to the front, she's got her ribbon hat off and the corn suit in her hands. The top, yellow part is flopped over in front, and she steps one foot into the green bottom half through its open back.

"Hey," I tell her, "don't you want to play games? And win prizes?"

She picks up her other foot, but doesn't put it into the suit yet. "I want prizes," she says.

"Well, then we have to go back down to the games. It's getting late and we're not allowed on the midway after dark. You know that—Mom's rules."

"I want to win prizes," Andrew says.

Lou-Ann lines up next to Andrew.

Penny pulls her first foot out of the corn suit. "Can I be a corn later, Mr. Caffrey?"

"Of course you may, Penny," her teacher says.

She hands the corn suit to another kid and skips over to Lou-Ann and Andrew's we-want-to-play-games-and-win-prizes line.

I pull Lewis a couple of steps away and tell him my plan for our five-thirty break.

"Here you go, Miller." Penny's teacher leans out and hands me a paper boat full of samples. "Take these for yourselves, as a thank-you for lending us your dad. Butter?"

"Plain is perfect, Mr. Caffrey," I say. "Thanks!"

I'm so happy to have this key item from my Fair food plan in my hand that I don't even care if it's a bunch of two-inch-long chunks instead of a whole corn on the cob. I cradle the paper boat against my chest. Sweet steam tickles my nose. My check-in strategy worked, I have Holmsbury Elementary corn, and I also have a plan to fix the pie disaster. I'm finally making progress in the *right* direction. Positive momentum.

"Miller!" my dad calls from the back. "Andrew's mother just called. She'll be here between five thirty and six."

More positive momentum! I put my hand on Penny's shoulder.

"Train formation," I tell the others. "Hold onto the person in front of you. Single file." The paths are packed solid and I'm not taking any chances.

Lou-Ann is our engine, then Andrew, Lewis, Penny, and I'm the caboose. Three steps later, one of the two billion other people on the Fair path bulldozes into my elbow. *Wham!* The corn samples flip into the air. I lunge sideways, jut my arm out, and snatch a single chunk of corn in mid-flight with the empty paper boat. The other five pieces hit the ground and roll away in a forest of feet.

"Hold it," I yell. I let go of Penny and scrape all the corn from the cob in four bites.

"The spirits are warning you," Lewis chants like Postrenika. "Stay away from flying death heads." He tilts his head in the direction of the graveyard fence.

"Very funny," I say. "Anyway, I told you I'm finished with flying death heads."

"You already went on the Flying Death Heads ride?" Penny asks.

I roll my eyes. "It's *not* a ride," I tell her. "And quit eavesdropping."

22
LIFE SCIENCE

Back on the midway, the four of us with money left each give Lou-Ann one of our dollars so she can play games. We throw Ping-Pong balls into fish bowls, pop balloons with darts, and toss rings onto milk bottles. Lewis and I watch while Penny, Andrew, and Lou-Ann fish rubber duckies out of the plastic pool to win tiny plastic prizes. Then they watch Lewis and me climb to the top of the shaky, almost-horizontal rope ladder without flipping it to try and win a big prize. I tip over on the second rung and Lewis tips on the third rung and we don't win any prizes at all. Playing all of those games took about eleven minutes.

"Let's do the Kentucky Derby race," Lewis suggests. "There're only five squirt-gun stations in the whole game. Since there are five of us, one of us'll come in first and win."

"I'll get the rest of my money." Andrew turns his pocket inside out and extracts an ancient, lint-covered lollipop and two dimes.

Penny pulls her pockets inside out. They're empty.

Lewis and I split the cost of the Derby game for everybody. My pocket now contains three dollars and fifty cents. According to my sad Fair calculations, this means I went on two rides (if you count the House of Mirrors), played eleven minutes' worth of games plus the upcoming Derby, and ate half of a colossal sugar donut for thirty-nine dollars and fifty cents. Forget the baseball cap—I don't even have enough left for any kind of birthday present for my mom.

We line up at the squirt guns, and the Derby guy sounds the bell.

"And they're off!" he yells.

Lewis is more interested in shooting his movie than shooting his squirt gun, so his racehorse doesn't make much progress along the track. I press my trigger only part of the time so I won't win. We walk away from the midway with three blow-up crayons, one tiny purple giraffe, five spider rings, one empty bottle of bubbles that Andrew won then spilled into the rubber ducky pond, three live goldfish in plastic bags, and the large green stuffed dog Lou-Ann's horse won in the Derby.

It's six minutes past five. We still have some time before I can drop the first-graders with my dad and run to adult baking. Across the field, the sun is sinking toward the tops

of the trees. The music from the midway is fading behind us, replaced by moos, baas, and cock-a-doodle-doos.

"I want to see the animals," Penny says.

"Me too," Andrew pipes up.

The animal barns sit all in a row along the path that leads away from the midway. There's a barn for sheep and pigs, one for goats and llamas, and one for rabbits and poultry. On the poultry side of the barn, chickens, ducks, turkeys, and crazy-looking roosters with feathers sticking up out of their heads all stare at you sideways with beady black eyes. The first animal barn is the Cow Palace, which they call a "palace" to pretend it doesn't smell. When we walk through the big open doorway, my nose is not fooled.

I look around for Bailey from our class, but I don't see her and I don't see her prize-winning black-and-white cow Cosette, either. Rows and rows of other cows are standing or lying down in hay-filled stalls. Up close they look huge. There's a lot of mooing. We watch a small boy lead an acorn-colored cow around a show ring by its rope halter.

"C'mon, Bucky," he says. "Atta girl, Bucky."

The cow's tail swishes back and forth. Judges sit at a table and make notes on clipboards as Bucky circles the ring.

Lou-Ann runs across the barn toward a mob in the corner. Penny and Andrew follow her and they wiggle-worm between and under people to get to the front. For a mob, this one is oddly quiet. There's a little whispering, but that's all.

"MILLER!" I hear my sister yell. "IT'S A BABY COW! IT WAS BORN HERE LAST NIGHT!"

"SHHHHHH!" people hiss.

I slink backwards, hoping no one I know is nearby, and by nearby I mean closer than Mars. I think about changing my name.

"It is you," Bailey says, coming around the crowd. "Hi. Hey, Lewis. Come see Cosette's new calf."

She leads us to a rope divider and holds it up so we can duck underneath. I see Penny and the others kneeling at the edge of the rope. Bailey's dad, sitting in a folding chair near the wall, looks up from his book and nods at us.

Cosette is lying in a thick bed of clean hay. Lewis raises his camera and she blinks her long cow lashes at him. Her black-and-white sides bulge, and we can see the knobby bones of her spine. On the other side of her huge bulk, a calf snuggles against her. It's a little bigger than Cooper. The fur on its head curls in silky wisps, with pink skin showing through the white parts.

"Wow," I whisper to Bailey. "Were you here when it was born?"

"I always stay with Cosette at the Fair. I sleep here. Last night I helped pull while she pushed."

"Cool!" Lewis says. "That would've made a great Fair scene! Was it gross?"

"A little." Bailey grins.

"What's its name?" I ask.

"Mr. Mistoffelees," she says. "You can come over to our farm next week and pat him. Right now only Cosette can touch him, so he'll know she's his mom." She glances toward the crowd on the other side of the ropes.

The calf nuzzles his mother's belly.

"No fair!" Penny grouses in a whisper that would register in the warning zone of a noise meter. "I want to be inside the ropes, too!"

I remember to check my watch. Five twenty. This is it. Time to dump the first-graders and put my pie plan into action. "I've got to go," I tell Bailey. "Thanks for letting us see Cosette's new calf."

23
STRONG FORCES

"I don't want to go all the way up to the corn stand again," Penny complains. "It's too far to carry our prizes.

We're almost there," I tell her. "Stop dragging. We can't be late."

Just a little farther up the hill. Then Lewis and I will speed straight to adult baking on our own. I'll get there before my dad does, fix the pie problem, and finally, *finally* my worries will be over. And at six, I might be off Pest patrol for good. I blow out a big breath. Lewis nods from behind his flip-out screen because he knows what I'm thinking.

"Here's the youth exhibit!" Andrew shouts. "I want to see my mini go-kart."

"Yeah!" my sister says. "I want to see my painting, and my doll blanket, and my pear butter, and my—"

"Look, we can't stop now," I tell them. An idea bursts into my brain. "Tell Dad you want to go to the youth exhibit, and he'll bring you right back here the minute we meet up with him."

And he won't be able to head over to adult baking. Brilliant! Lewis makes a thumbs-up sign for my eyes only. I stride across the Fair path and along the wooden storm fence to the corn kitchen. Our blue backpack is leaning against a hay bale just inside the fence, and I reach over to retrieve it. Lewis and I let the air out of the blow-up crayons and stash them with the rest of the prizes in the backpack—even the fish, who have lots of air in their bags and will probably be much happier resting in the shade. Penny and the others make fangs out of bits of hay.

"We're here, Dad," I call.

He's hunched over another spread of appliance parts.

"Thanks, Miller. But hey, I'm sorry," he says. "I've got to get this thermostat up and running. I can't take time off right now."

"But Dad!" I burst out. "Come *on*! I need to—"

"And...*cut*." Lewis kicks the side of my foot. I shut up.

"It was only a five-minute break, anyway," Dad says. "I promise you'll be off on your own at six. Just another half-hour."

My whole body sags. This has to be the most unfair Friday in the history of the Holmsbury Fair.

"Oh!" Dad looks up. "Andrew's mother called back. She

asked you to meet her at the youth exhibit at six. I'll come down, too, so you and Penny can just wait for me there."

"Okay," I say.

"I'll come straight there. Unless"—Dad wiggles his eyebrows at me—"you want to meet me at the adult baking exhibit so we can see my pi—"

"Youth exhibit's good," I say quickly, glancing at Penny. She's not paying attention. Close one, I think.

I come up with one last, desperate plan. As soon as Dad gets to the youth exhibit I'll tear straight up the hill to adult baking. I have to get to the judges ahead of him. It's my last lemon meringue hope.

24
ALBERT EINSTEIN LEAVES THE BUILDING

"Hiya, Miller," Mrs. Noyes says. She's sitting at the entrance to the youth exhibit drinking a Holmsbury Library lemonade. "Way to go on your entry this year!"

I smile, but since Mrs. Noyes would say "way to go" even for a "nice try" ribbon, I don't get my hopes up. For extra luck, I decide to look at everything else before I check out my Theory of Everything "collection."

Penny, Andrew, and Lou-Ann scatter to look for their entries. "Stay right here in this building until my dad and Andrew's mom get here," I call after them.

Since the youth exhibit is one long barn with a divider in the middle and only the one door, Lou-Ann can't disappear in here. And since there are no moving parts in the barn and there's nothing to eat, even Andrew ought to be able to keep himself in one piece. I can't believe I made it through this whole, mostly awful Fair day without losing one member of the Pest Pack, but I did it. I let out a big, long breath.

"Want to see my entry?" Lewis asks.

"Sure," I tell him. "You did photos, right?"

"Well, I wanted to print some stills off of my last movie but we were out of photo paper. So I picked wildflowers at the last minute."

We walk over to the flower display, a wall of long shelves right near the front of the youth exhibit. Lewis shows me his entry, a tall vase exploding with flowers in every shape and color. There's a blue ribbon next to it and a purple rosette with purple and gold ribbons streaming down from it.

"You got a first place *and* a special!" I thump him on the back. "Good going!"

"Can you believe that?" Lewis grins. "So where's your Theory of Everything? I looked for it this morning, but I couldn't find it with the sculptures."

"It's not in the sculptures," I say. "I'll show you when we get to it. Let's just start from here and walk around the barn."

We examine the tinfoil constructions, the dioramas, and the toilet-paper-roll robots. Lewis pans along the row of decorated pumpkins set up at the foot of the artwork wall.

"I like those three white pumpkins stacked to make a

snowman." I point. "And the one that's a chicken."

"I had this great idea for decorating a pumpkin," Lewis says. "I was gonna cut out the insides and make it into an aquarium, with blue cellophane and papier-mâché fish you could see from the outside."

"But you can't cut or poke the pumpkins or they'll rot during the Fair," I tell him. "I read that in the Fair handbook."

"Yeah," Lewis says, "that's why I didn't do it. Hey—your sister's drawing got a red!"

"That's good. She did work pretty hard on it."

Lewis cranes his neck, peering around the corner. "A kid down there is giving a whittling demonstration—looks like he's making a walking stick. That would make a good close-up. Want to come?"

Woodworking is a lot closer to the collections than we are now, and even though I'm not superstitious like Lewis, I don't want to jinx my project by going out of order. "I'll be there in a bit," I say.

"Okay. I'll be back." Lewis walks away.

"Miller! There you are!"

Andrew's mother hurries over to me all out of breath. My watch says a quarter to six, my brain says adult baking exhibit, and I start breathing faster myself.

"What a day I've had!" she exclaims. "First that terrible migraine. Then I took this new medicine that knocked me flat. I can't believe I slept the whole day away. And you walked all the kids to the Fair by yourself! How did you do it? How have things been going here?"

"Okay," I say, speaking for Andrew and the others, not for myself. "We—"

"It was such a challenge getting here," she goes on. "The traffic is backed up all the way to Wellstown. I had to park at the lower shuttle bus lot. Thank goodness I feel so much better now. And thank *you* for your note, and for stepping in like you did. Where are the little guys? Lou-Ann's mom couldn't get here, so I'm bringing Lou-Ann home, too."

Yahoo! Two down, and one to go! "They're here," I say, "looking at their—"

"It's too bad your mom had that emergency today, Miller," Andrew's mother says. "She missed the whole day at the Fair, just like me. Oh wait." She rummages around inside her gigantic yellow purse. "Here's Lou-Ann's ten dollars. You must have paid for her ride bracelet. Or your dad did. So nice of you. I was holding it for her and I forgot all about it. I blame that migraine headache. What a day!"

"Mommy!" Andrew squeaks. He trips into his mother and throws his arms around her. "Come see my go-kart!"

Penny and Lou-Ann want her to come see their entries, too.

"Okay," she says. "Once around and then it's time to go home. Except for you, Penny. When we're done looking, you'll stay here with your brother."

They move off down one side of the youth exhibit so that now I'm completely not in charge. Finally. I pump my fist in the air. I should go have a look at my project, but, putting it off, I backtrack to get a closer look at the decorated cakes.

One cake looks like a swimming pool. It has a cookie diving board and blue Jell-O in the middle for water. The cake next to it is a realistic-looking hamburger cake with lettuce, tomatoes, and mustard made of colored icing. Unlike a "physics collection," a decorated cake is a regular entry category in the Fair handbook. I should try that category next year—Dad can teach me how to bake, and the decorating part seems fun. That's *if* Dad still loves to bake after today. I gulp.

Andrew appears at my elbow. His mom and the others are standing behind him.

"Thanks for taking me to the Fair," he mumbles.

"Tell Miller what you told me, Andrew," his mother prompts.

Andrew stares straight ahead and recites, "If I had to have a big brother you wouldn't be a bad one."

"That's what you think," Penny says.

Lou-Ann smiles at me, then looks at her pink boots.

"Let's go, kids," Andrew's mother says. "Thanks again, Miller, and please thank Lewis again for us, too." She hustles Andrew and Lou-Ann through the doorway. "Bye-bye!"

"You're welcome," I say, even though they're already out the door.

Penny runs after them. "I'll give you your prizes tomorrow," she calls. She comes back. "I won A LOT of ribbons," she tells me.

I glance down at my watch. Ten minutes to six. "Why don't you go look at them again while we wait for Dad?" I suggest.

"Good idea!" She hops away along the row of display cases.

Now that I've taken care of Penny for the next six hours, I check out the rest of the displays, working my way toward the collections. I don't see Lewis near the whittler so I figure he must be shooting somewhere else. I look at other kids' entries while I try to come up with something convincing to say to the adult baking judges. I have nine minutes.

At the far end of the building, I see a girl climb up the railing that protects the entries from the hordes of Fair-goers in the youth exhibit. I'm sure whoever is watching that kid will tell her to get down because you're not supposed to be on the railings. Then I realize the climber is my sister.

Unbelieveable! Nine minutes left to solve the pie problem and I have to waste them worrying about Pain-elope. I stomp one step toward her, then stop. Actually, I don't have to take care of this problem. There are always committee members watching the exhibit, so I'll just let someone from the youth committee get Painy off of the railing. No one even knows I'm with her. I turn around and start to walk the other way.

"MILLER!" she yells. "MILLER YOU HAVE TO COME HERE RIGHT NOW!"

No, I don't! I've spent all day keeping track of Painy and her friends, and I'm *not* going over to her now. In fact, I'm not even staying in the building with her. I barge around the divider the other way and up to the front entrance. When I get outside, I fold my arms and face uphill with my back to the youth exhibit. Dad can't get here soon enough for me.

People are moving in and out of the horticulture building, the photography building, and the crafts building in a thick, steady stream. There are probably lots of people in adult baking, too, I realize. How long it will take me to find the judges? What if they're not even there anymore?

I look back at the door to the youth exhibit. Lewis is in there shooting video. Penny knows Dad is on his way, and she's waiting to show him her ribbons. Adult baking is just up the hill, so why should I wait until I have to race Dad there at six? I can check out the pie situation and try to find the judges right now, instead of during my time off. That way, when Dad gets to the youth exhibit I'll be free and clear—my pie worries will be taken care of, Dad can go see his entry, and Lewis and I can do the rest of the Fair on our own like every other Holmsbury sixth grader. *Finally!*

I weave through the solid wall of people in front and push past the horticulture building toward the fence. If I slip behind the buildings I can make better time.

Near the fence, a tall, skinny figure is leaning against a light pole.

"Enjoying the Fair, Murray?"

I stop short.

"Um...sort of," I tell Rip. Questions start to ping around in my brain. Why does he keep turning up? And is it just a coincidence that he's next to the fence that separates the Fair from the old graveyard?

"Only *sort of* enjoying the Fair? Well, well." Rip peers at me from under his white eyebrows. He chuckles. "And how about those flying death heads? Seen any of those lately?"

A chill prickles down my spine. *Lewis was right!* Rip *is* trying to get me into the old graveyard! Is Lewis right about him being a ghost, too? I wish Lewis was here so we could try to collect more ghosts-on-video data. But he's not. So what should I do? My mind races.

Ghost matter shouldn't feel like regular person matter. And if ghosts exist in a different dimension then you shouldn't be able to feel them at all.

I take a step toward Rip, reach my hand toward his arm, brace myself, and—

A trumpet fanfare blares over the loudspeakers.

"That's my cue." Rip strides up the hill. "See you later, Manley."

Just before Rip disappears into the moving mob, I see the woman in the long dress join him. Then they're gone.

"Miller," I mumble, slumping against the light pole.

I have no new data for Lewis, and now it's three minutes to six. It's too late to make it to adult baking and back in time. My last and worst pie plan is all I have left. The second I see my dad, I'll blast off for adult baking.

I go back into the youth exhibit to tell Lewis he was right about Rip trying to get me into the graveyard. When I pass the collections display, I stop. I never checked to see what the judges thought of my entry. First, I see a collection of pencils with all of the names of the states on them. It has won a red ribbon. There's a collection of miniature train engines with a blue ribbon. There are bottle caps (yellow ribbon), fancy toothpicks (yellow ribbon), foreign coins, and stamps (red and blue).

I find my "physics collection" hanging on the side wall just above the railing. It has not won any ribbon at all. None. Not even a light green "nice try" ribbon. How could the judges do that? I know my Theory of Everything isn't a collection, but I worked so hard on it. And I added all of those extra-great models—the pompom bow, the garnet rock, the dead June beetle, Albert—

WHAT?

I lean over the railing. I'm staring at an empty space on my corkboard. *Where is Albert Einstein?* Maybe he fell off. I check the bottom shelf of the display case. There are other collections and lots of ribbons. But my bendable Albert Einstein is gone!

Painy! I saw her climb on the railing. She could have

taken him then. I start a slow burn. She was also in the car with my project by herself last night before we left for the fairgrounds. I never even looked inside the box when I handed in my entry. No wonder I didn't get a ribbon. My project is missing its best part!

"What's wrong?" Lewis asks, coming up.

"Have you seen my sister? I need to talk to her *right now*."

He shakes his head "Uh-uh. I've been shooting near the back." He taps his camera. "She must be farther down the row, or on the other side of the building."

"You go that way, I'll go this way." I point. "Meet me at the front when you find her."

I run through one side of the youth exhibit. There are tons of kids and parents here. No Penny. When I get to the front, Lewis is there. By himself.

"She's in here somewhere," I say through gritted teeth. "Try again. Full circle each."

We don't find her.

"She took Albert Einstein off of my project!" I exclaim. "She didn't just disappear!"

Lewis thinks back. "I saw her near the whittling. After that I shot the doorway action for a while." He snaps his fingers. "If she left the building, then I should have it."

He flips out the camera screen and hits fast rewind. We scan the replay of people coming and going through the wide youth exhibit entrance. Nothing. Lewis runs it back and plays it again.

“There!” he says. He stops the camera, rewinds, and plays it in slow motion.

People move in and out of the youth exhibit at one-quarter speed. A big jam-up clogs the entrance for a second or two. Then a splash of Fair ribbons weaves through the clog and out of the building.

My worry meter starts to flicker.

25
A SATELLITE OUT OF ORBIT

"Where could your sister be? And why would she take Albert Einstein?" Lewis asks.

"Who knows how her brain works?" I squint, trying to let my mind follow the convoluted Pain-elope process. "She wanted to play with him last night. Maybe she took him outside to show him the Fair."

We go outside and check around near the entrance to the youth exhibit. Kids are chasing each other, adults are sitting on benches, and the library volunteers are selling lemonade from the cart across the way. My sister isn't there.

"She knows my dad is meeting us here. She can't have gone far," I tell Lewis. "I'll find her."

"Your dad'll be here any second," Lewis says. "Should I wait for him?"

"That would be good. Our mom always tells us to go to the corn stand if we get separated. If I don't find Penny right around here, I'll go up there and meet her." On the other side of the lemonade cart, I see the red and black checked shirt again.

"Turn on your camera!" I grab Lewis's arm. "There's Rip!"

A bunch of little kids barrels out of the youth exhibit into us. Lewis cradles his camera to his chest.

"Wait, kids!" a dad calls, running after them.

I push past the lemonade cart and scour the area. "We missed him again," I say. "I wish you and your camera had been with me when I saw him a couple of minutes ago. He asked me if I'd seen the flying death heads. He met a woman in an old-fashioned dress after he walked away. That's the second time I saw her, too."

Lewis gapes. *"You saw one of the Maynard sisters?"*

"I don't know about them, but right now I'd better go get *my* sister. Tell my dad where I went, okay?"

I speed walk up and down the paths, looking in every direction. Wouldn't it be just like Penny to ruin my last chance to get to the pie judges before my dad? At least that dumb ribbon hat should help me pick her out of the crowd.

After circling around the area four times, I come to the conclusion that my sister and her hat are not near the youth exhibit. I sprint at Mach speed to the corn stand. She isn't there. Mrs. Delgado, my fourth-grade teacher, is in the front selling corn.

"Excuse me, Mrs. D., but have you seen my sister, Penny?" I ask her.

"Hi, Miller! You know, I might have seen her partway down the hill a few minutes ago." Mrs. Delgado purses her lips, thinking. "Is she wearing a colorful hat?"

"That's her. Thanks." Heading downhill, I search the area on and near the path. No ribbon hat. I hurry back to Mrs. Delgado. "If she comes here again, would you please have her wait for me? She took—er—we got separated."

"Of course," Mrs. D. says. "Lots of families meet up here. Maybe she just stopped in the restroom first. Have you checked?"

Good idea, I think.

I run partway down the hill to the cinderblock bathroom building. My sister isn't in the part of the line that stretches out the door. I'm not about to walk into a women's bathroom, so I hang around near the door and wait to see if she comes out. She doesn't. I check my watch. Six fifteen. Where *is* she?

The sun is sinking behind the far hills. Streaks of hot pink and orange color the sky. The hordes of people moving up, down, and across the fairgrounds are fading to gray. My worry meter has risen into the yellow zone.

I squeeze my eyes shut and try to concentrate. Why would Penny run off? She might zip out of the youth exhibit to say hi to someone, but she'd come back. She can't have gone to buy a treat or play a game because she doesn't have any money. What else would she want to do?

I open my eyes and watch the waves of people moving in and out of the animal barns at the bottom of the hill. Signs for the food stands light up, one after another. A big neon sign winks on: "COW PALACE." *Wait a minute!* She wanted to get under the ropes to see Bailey's new calf. That's one place she could be.

I hurtle down the grassy part of the hill, past the picnic tables and the stage where the high school show choir is singing and dancing in the growing dusk. I duck between some food carts, cross the path, and run straight through the barn doors of the Cow Palace.

"Excuse me...sorry...excuse me," I say. I elbow my way through the crowd of calf watchers whispering in the back corner.

When Bailey's dad sees me, he shakes his head. "Bailey's watching the show choir," he says. "She's not here."

"That's okay," I tell him. "I'm looking for my sister."

"The loud one? Haven't seen her."

"Oh, okay. Thanks anyway." I leave the Cow Palace at six twenty-two.

"ATTENTION PLEASE!" the loudspeaker blares. "PENELOPE SANFORD, PLEASE COME TO THE CORN STAND. PENELOPE SANFORD TO THE HOLMSBURY ELEMENTARY CORN STAND." A short trumpet blast follows.

When I hear the announcement, I know my dad has been to the youth exhibit and has talked to Lewis. I know he's been to the corn stand and from there, to the Fair

Office. I can picture him now, running back to the corn stand to wait for Penny. If she doesn't show up there in a few minutes, all of the Fair security people will start looking for her.

I think about how upset my mom was about the girl who ran away and my own worry meter surges through orange and up into the red zone. If it isn't safe for that missing teenager to be out on her own, then it's a trillion times worse for Penny. The sun is going down, the Fair is full of strangers, and my six-year-old sister is out there somewhere on her own.

Bringing those little kids here was a bad idea. And not because I couldn't go on any fun rides or eat basically anything, or because we had to walk the whole way and they spent all my money and kept wandering off into the crowds like satellites out of orbit.

It was a bad idea because I wasn't responsible or careful. I only had seven minutes to go and one six-year-old left to watch. The last one. Just my own little sister. I brought her, and I left her, and now she's lost at the Fair. Fingers of ice run up my arms and neck and down my back.

The Last One. I have a pretty good idea of where to look for Penny.

26
ANOTHER DIMENSION

I rocket up the hill. My legs are burning, but I don't slow down. I wasted hours today worrying that Penny would tell my dad that his pie got eaten up. But she heard me talking about something else—*somewhere* else she thought was much more interesting. She told me she wanted to go there. *Twice!* I have to find her, and I can't waste another minute.

I veer into the grassy alley next to the souvenir shop. A rectangle of light spills out of a window high in the building's cement wall. Dusk has crept in beyond. I kick through a pile of empty boxes, then I'm at the fence.

Squeezing my body through the gap feels even tighter tonight. Edges of the chain link scratch my arms. I push myself up onto my feet and scan the graveyard. But I don't see anyone, just the dark shapes of all those trees, bushes, and gravestones against the dimming sky.

Penny doesn't even go upstairs in our house alone at night when all the lamps are *on*. It was probably lighter when she first came here to look for the flying death heads "ride," but it's pretty dark and gloomy now. It's getting colder, too, and her sweatshirt is still in our backpack.

I take a deep breath and strike out between the rows of stones. I walk up and down, calling, "Penny! Penny are you here?" Mixed with the Fair music and noise, my voice sounds strange and thin.

I hear a faint noise in the distance. "P-Penny?" No answer. I half expect to see hundred-year-old Rip materialize in front of me. He doesn't. And now I'm not sure I heard anything, either. I keep checking all around the graveyard. The sounds of the Fair seem very far away.

Wishing I wasn't, I'm thinking about ghosts again. Could a ghost cross into our dimension? *Would* he? I look over my shoulder, then keep going.

"Penny!" I call.

Cold air seeps through my shirt. I shiver. I'm standing in front of three short headstones in a row, tilting at odd angles. I see the wings of a flying death head on the closest one. I can just make out the small stone I tripped on last night—*The Last One*.

I hear rustling sounds, coming closer. "P-Penny?"

What if Lewis is right? Is Rip the ghost of the carriage driver? Maybe he's helping the Maynards find their youngest sister! And is Lewis right about the woman in the long dress,

too? A terrible idea slams into me. Rip didn't want to get *me* into the graveyard. He used me to get *Penny* here—so that Maynard sister I saw could take Penny for her lost sister!

Now I definitely hear a swishing sound. It's very close. My teeth chatter.

I hear a high-pitched, raspy whisper: "*Miller!*"

A figure rises up from behind one of the gravestones.

"She's MY sister!" I yell. "You can't have her!"

"*Miller!*"

I'm not waiting around for ghosts. I stumble through the rows of graves, lurching toward the lights of the Fair. When I reach the fence, I dive for the hole. Halfway through, something catches me.

I struggle. I thrash. "Let go!" I cry.

Riiiip!

I pitch onto the ground on the Fair side of the fence and scramble to my feet, already running.

"Miller, wait! It's me!"

I stop short in the grassy alley and turn.

"Lewis?" I gasp.

27
SIX-YEAR-OLD-SISTER MOLECULES

Lewis catches up and we hurry out of the alley and down the hill.

"I...thought you...were a ghost!" I gasp. "What are you doing in the graveyard? You said you'd never go there again!" I rub my back through the gaping hole in my T-shirt.

"Yeah. Rest in peace," he says. "But Penny kept asking about the flying death heads. You thought of that, too, right?"

I nod. "It was a good idea. But she wasn't there."

He stops and flips open his camera screen. "I've gotta show you something."

I try to focus on the small lump of stone in the middle of the shaky frame.

"Is it the grave of The Last One?" I say.

"Keep looking."

A hand appears in the video. It's Lewis's. He pushes the grass down at the base of the stone as the camera zooms in: Almira Maynard 1761.

"The last Maynard sister is already buried there. Not missing." Lewis closes the camera.

"Wow," I say. "Okay. *She's* not missing, but *my* sister still is. Unless my dad's found her," I add, hopefully.

"Don't think so." Lewis reaches into his pocket. "I got my brother to give me his cell phone. Your dad'll call when he finds her."

I check the glowing dial of my watch. "A quarter to seven! If my mom gets here and we don't have Penny—" I can't even finish the thought.

"Right," Lewis says. "Where should we look?"

I cross my arms and hug them to my chest, shivering a little. "She could be anywhere by now."

"Would she go to any of the adult exhibits?" Lewis asks. "She likes to draw. How about artwork?" He stops at the entrance to the art and crafts building.

"Maybe. You go there, and I'll check photography. Meet me at the front of the photography building in five minutes."

We split up. I cut behind the onion rings cart and hurry into photography. The aisles in the narrow white barn are thick with people. I sidle around the room, making sure I look in every corner.

I feel a tug on my shirt. "You're Penny's brother," a little girl says. "I saw you at the Mini-Swings. She's in my class."

Her dad smiles at me, then goes back to examining a large close-up of a hummingbird.

"Oh, um, good," I say, edging away. I don't have time to *chat* about Penny right now. I have to *find* her.

"I saw her hat with the ribbons," the girl says.

Who could miss it? I think. I move toward the door.

"It looked funny on that pumpkin witch," the girl calls after me.

"What?" I say. I whirl in time to see the girl and her dad go into the small, dark room for the slide show.

I run outside and find Lewis.

"A kid from Penny's class just told me she saw that stupid ribbon hat on a pumpkin that was decorated like a witch," I tell him. "We have to go back to the youth exhibit."

"Back to the scene of the crime," he says, "like in a detective movie."

At the youth exhibit, we examine the decorated pumpkins lined up along the artwork wall. We check all the way down the row and back, twice. There are three pumpkins decorated like witches. One is a whole witch, with hands, feet, and a cape. Two are witches' heads. They're all wearing pointy black hats.

"No ribbon hat," I say. "Now what?"

"Where was the last place you saw her?" Lewis asks.

"Climbing on the railing next to my project." I check my watch and let out a groan. "That was a whole hour ago!"

We dash around the divider to the collections. I keep my eyes on the doorway, trying to make air molecules rearrange themselves into six-year-old-sister molecules. It doesn't work.

"I thought you said she took Albert Einstein." Lewis points to the wall.

Albert is back on the corkboard, looking a little crooked and slightly grubby.

"How did he get back here?" My brain is scrambling. "And if he's here, then where's Penny?"

We rush back to the doorway of the youth exhibit.

"Are you still looking for your sister, Miller?" Mrs. Noyes looks up from her desk near the door. "She was in here a little while ago. She said she was waiting for your dad. That was just before they announced her name on the loudspeaker."

"Was she wearing a hat?" I ask.

"The one she made with all of her ribbons?" Mrs. Noyes thinks a second. "Yes," she nods, "I think she was."

Lewis and I hurry outside. He takes out his brother's phone and checks it. No calls.

"Well, she's not with your dad at the corn stand. Maybe she doesn't listen to the announcements," Lewis says.

"She told Mrs. Noyes she was waiting here." I look all around in front of the youth exhibit doorway.

"I'll go this way." Lewis points uphill. "You go the other way. Meet back here in two minutes." He takes off.

I take a step, then stop. A solid mass of people surges as far as I can see—down, up, and across the hillside, and in and out of every building and exhibit. Bright neon signs and flashing midway rides make everything around them disappear. Electronic squawks, bells, blaring music, shouts, and animal sounds swamp the shadows. I don't feel one tiny bit of the Fair force field anywhere around me now. Instead the Fair feels huge, dark, and chaotic, filled with hidden traps into which a small six-year-old sister could vanish without a trace.

I can't even think of where to look first. Everything here—every blade of grass, every cow, every Firefighter fry—is a collection of the same subatomic strings, and my sister is, too. Instead of helping, particle physics is making me think the search is hopeless and I'll never find her again as long as I live.

I take a breath. I remind myself that the different ways those subatomic strings wiggle is what makes them into Penny, from her hopping Penny feet to her impossible-to-follow Penny ideas. The *same* strings, but *different* motion, I think. The *same*, but *different*.

I move to the edge of the circle of light spilling from the youth exhibit doorway. Just across the pavement, lots of people are waiting in line for lemonade. Beyond them I can barely make out the picket fence around the giant pumpkin patch.

Lewis comes back.

"No luck," he says. "Anyway, how could that girl have

seen the ribbon hat on one of those witch pumpkins if Mrs. Noyes saw Penny wearing it when she left the youth exhibit?"

The *same*, but *different*, I think again. *One of those witch pumpkins?* I grab Lewis by the arm and pull him past the lemonade cart. "Come on!" I say. "We've got to check the *giant* pumpkins!"

We zigzag between people on the Fair path, dart inside the gate, and work our way through all of the people milling around the pumpkin patch. The giant jack-o'-lanterns are lined up in a row at the far side.

"She's not there," Lewis says. "We can see she's not there."

"We can't think like us," I tell him. "We have to think like Penny." What was it my sister said about the giant jack-o'-lanterns? I search for her exact words. *I wanted to go the whole way inside.*

"Inside a giant pumpkin!" I shout.

We bolt across the grass.

I charge around the picket fence, examining the giant jack-o'-lanterns from the front. Lewis checks the back. Some have been carved like the faces of cartoon characters. One has a pointy-toothed cat, arched and hissing at a bat. Another jack-o'-lantern looks like Frankenstein. Two are witches. They're lit with electric lights, and we can see right through to their hollow, Creamsicle-colored insides. Penny isn't in any of them.

"The space inside those pumpkins is pretty small, Mill," Lewis says.

"Penny is small." I slump against a tent pole. "She's only six."

Lewis turns his camera on and off. "Well," he says glumly, "it was worth a try."

On the dark outskirts of the pumpkin patch, I see giant hunks of rind and piles of seeds and slop. A couple of partially-carved giant pumpkins have been abandoned back

there, too. One of them has something on top of it. I move a few steps closer.

"I saved Albert Einstein," one half-carved jack-o'-lantern says. It has a one-eyed, grinning witch face. And it's wearing a ribbon hat.

28
RUNNING AT SUPERSONIC SPEED

"Penny!" I shout. When I see her unfold out of the back of the jack-o'-lantern, my throat clogs. I grab her in a hug, then immediately let go.

"Yecch!"

Her skin and her clothes are sticky. She smells like pumpkin goo. She puts her ribbon hat on, then takes a handful of slimy pumpkin seeds out of her pocket.

"I'm going to plant a giant jack-o'-lantern," she tells me.

"Okay," I say. My voice sounds a little wavery.

"We've got her, Mr. Sanford." Lewis has already called my dad. "She's fine. Sure." He puts the phone back in his pocket. "Your dad's meeting us at Library lemonade," he says.

We walk across the path. I hold my sister's slimy hand and don't let go.

"We've been looking everywhere for you!" I tell her.

"And what do you mean, you *saved Albert Einstein?*"

"Well," Penny says. She looks at me and at Lewis to make sure we're paying attention. Which we are. "I saw a baby in a backpack thing reach out and grab at a collection. So I climbed up the railing to see what it was. And I saw that your project had an empty spot where that clay person was supposed to be."

We sit down on the bench opposite the lemonade cart.

"Actually," she explains to Lewis, "the clay person was more of a lumpy toad."

I sigh.

"The baby was holding something with whitish fuzzy hair." She pokes me in the chest. "You stuck Albert Einstein on your project. Just like I told you to!"

I look at the sky and count to a zillion.

"So...," Lewis prompts.

"So the baby's parents went right out of the building, and Albert Einstein is Miller's favorite." She looks at me. "I called you, but you didn't answer."

"I know. I'm sorry," I say. Which I truly am.

"I had to run after them all over and even up the hill. I caught up right when that baby dropped Albert Einstein on the ground next to the picnic tables."

I picture Albert in his present state. "*You* pinned him back on my board?"

"Yes. And you weren't at the youth exhibit, and neither was Dad."

"So why didn't you go up to the corn stand like we're supposed to?"

"We were *supposed* to meet in the youth exhibit," Penny says, like I'm the one who changed the plan.

"But that was back at six—oh, never mind." I decide not to bother explaining the concept of time. "You didn't wait in the youth exhibit, either."

"Because I was waiting in the giant jack-o'-lantern," she says, as if that clears up everything.

"Kids!" Dad runs over and wraps Penny in his arms. He sniffs her. "I guess we know where you've been."

"I was helping Miller," she tells him.

"Helping Miller?"

"She was," I admit. "But not in the pumpkin." I give Dad the short version.

Dad wraps me in a hug that smells like corn, fries, and candy apples. "Good work finding Penny, Miller. This was a tough Fair Friday for all of us, I know. Yikes," he turns me around. "What happened to your shirt?"

"Long story," I say. I slip the blue backpack off of Dad's shoulder and dig out my sweatshirt. I hand Penny hers.

Chimpanzee laughter comes from Lewis's pocket. He answers the phone.

"My brother wants his phone back, and I have to go home," he tells us.

"You were a great buddy to all of us today, Lewis." Dad says. "Thanks!" He hugs Lewis, because it's that kind of night. "Mom's running a little late," he says, "Penny, let's you and I go see about our lemonade shift."

I walk Lewis a little ways up the path.

"I can't believe you hung in with me all day," I tell him.

"Action-packed, wasn't it?" he grins. "It's gonna make a great movie."

"What will you call it?"

"I'm leaning toward *The Holmsbury Fair Horror Show*."

I laugh.

"Nah—I can't come up with the real title until I figure out the story line." Lewis cocks his head, tapping one finger on his camera.

My dad and Penny come back from the lemonade cart.

"Hi! Hi, everybody!" Mom comes flying down the path. "Sorry I'm late. I hope you didn't worry!"

"We didn't worry about *you*," Dad says. He's still got one hand on Penny. "And we don't have to worry about working the lemonade cart, either, because they have extra lemon squeezers tonight."

"That's wonderful!" Mom says. "Now we can all be together!" More hugs all around. "Wait," she says. She holds Penny at arm's length. "What have you been into?"

"A pumpkin," my sister says. "But now I want to show you all of my new ribbons."

"I'll meet you at the youth exhibit in a couple of minutes," Dad says. "I have to see a guy about a pie." He grins and lopes up the hill.

Lewis and I stare at each other.

"Dad, wait!" I yell.

"Race you to adult baking," he calls over his shoulder.

I take off at supersonic speed.

29
A RUMPLED MESS OF MOLECULES

Dad is already inside the building when Lewis and I get there. He's examining the very front display case—the baking Court of Honor—and hasn't gone anywhere near the pie section yet.

Good, I think.

I have a minute, maybe two, to find the judges. But that's it. I turn toward the back of the building.

Lewis grabs my arm. He jerks his head at the baking Court of Honor. Fancy cakes and pies are on display inside the glass case—all blue-ribbon winners. One cake has a blue ribbon *and* a huge green and pink rosette ribbon for best in show.

"Lewis," I say under my breath. "I have to—"

He drags me to the glass. I stop breathing. Next to the best-in-show cake is my dad's pie dish. The last slice is gone; there's not a crumb left.

Bad, I think.

My heart sinks through the floor. I get the big joke now. A pie dish with no pie, in the baking Court of Honor.

Ha ha ha.

I swallow. I try to push words past the hunk of petrified wood in my throat. "Dad, I need to tell you—"

"Sure, in a sec, Miller. I want to see what the second note says."

Second note? There's more than one? My note is on a little stand to the left of the dish. I follow Dad's gaze to the right. There's another note. I lean close to the glass, and Lewis leans over my shoulder. We read:

Dear Mr. Sanford,

We couldn't award a place ribbon because your entry did not conform to the Fair handbook rules. After tasting the single remaining piece, however, we agree with your son's assessment: best ever. So we are awarding it the Judges' Choice, with our apologies for not leaving any of your delicious lemon meringue pie for display in its original baking dish.

Sincerely,
the Pie Judges

"Ha ha ha ho ho." Dad is laughing before I even finish reading. His blue, purple, and yellow Judges' Choice rosette is the biggest ribbon in the Court of Honor.

I feel like I might disintegrate into a rumpled mess of molecules on the spot.

Lewis points his camera at the notes. "Now *everybody* knows you're the king of pie, Mr. S.," he says.

"If I had known about the pie mix-up," Dad tells us, "I'd never have tried to enter that one last piece of pie. You're making saves all over the place today, Miller!"

"I thought you'd be mad, Dad," I admit.

"You should have told me, but hey"—he grabs my head in an armlock and pulls me in—"it's just pie. And I know you didn't set out to eat my Fair entry on purpose." He looks at his Judges' Choice ribbon again. "I had a feeling that old recipe I found in my great-grandmother's collection would be a winner. I should have written the name of the recipe on my entry form."

"What's it called?" I ask.

"Maynard's Meringue."

Lewis lowers his camera.

When we ran away from the flying death heads last night and showed up at adult baking just in time for the judges to go for coffee, I'd said, *Good thing the Maynard sisters scared us out of the graveyard.* But I was *joking!*

We stare at each other with our mouths open.

"What's with the two of you?" Dad says. "You look like you've just seen a ghost."

Lewis coughs. "Y-yeah, r-right, Mr. S.," he says.

The chimpanzee in his pocket laughs again.

"Oops," he says. "And…cut." He runs out of the building holding the phone to his ear.

"Thanks, Lewis." I watch him go.

That's it. My Fair Friday with Lewis is over. A long sigh leaks out of me.

"So," Dad says. "You had quite a job taking care of those kids, didn't you?"

"It looks easier when you and Mom do it," I admit.

Someone claps me on the shoulder. I turn, and the first thing I see is a red and black checked shirt. It's Rip! I fight off a shiver, activate my brain cells, and get ready to collect ghost matter data.

"The judges sure appreciated your note," Rip says with a chuckle.

I can feel his hand on my shoulder. There's weight, there's pressure, there are five regular person fingers.

"Hullo, Rip," Dad says. "Great Fair this year." They shake hands.

Dad sees him and hears him, and he can grip his hand. Okay, I think. "But who's the woman in the long dress?" I blurt out.

Rip gives me a quizzical look. "The woman in the…oh, you must mean my granddaughter Rose," Rip says. "Wasn't her display of antique baking tins in the Farm Museum interesting? And she sewed that old-fashioned costume herself," he adds proudly.

"Ohhh. A *costume*," I say. "It's—it's very nice."

Judges Choice
Physicists

Rip smiles a few thousand more wrinkles. "Thanks for all of your work setting up this week, Rob," he says. "Judges' choice and pie judge for next year, too. Not bad." He raises one of his shaggy eyebrows at me.

Based on my scientific observations and data, Rip does not seem to be a ghost. But he does seem to be waiting for me to say something.

"So…they gave Dad the ribbon *and* made him a judge?" I offer.

"Your dad gets the ribbon. The pie judge is *you*. Youngest baking judge in the history of the Fair. But watch yourself, Merwin," he warns. The old storyteller sits himself down on a bench and wags a long finger at me. "This all started for me with a note, too."

I feel a smile spread across my face. I put my hand under the neck of my sweatshirt and feel the "Rip" in my T-shirt. "A note *and* a hole in the fence," I say.

Rip lets out a big guffaw. Then he rearranges his wrinkles into a more serious expression. "Next year, you'll have to be here all Thursday afternoon and evening before the Fair," he says. "And you'll have to help judge the state bake-off on Saturday. You might as well come tomorrow at noon to see how that works. Judging's a big responsibility, you know."

"Tomorrow?" I risk a glance at Dad.

"My son is very responsible," he tells Rip. "He'll be here at noon tomorrow."

I don't jump up and down, even though I want to. "I'll be here," I say. *Very responsible*, I think. A Saturday job at the Fair!

"Are you a baking judge, too?" I ask Rip.

He laughs so hard all of his bones shake. "Someday, maybe, if I'm lucky," he manages, after a moment. "I'll have to check with my son, though. He's the boss in adult baking." He tips his head toward the hardware store owner, Mr. Hansen, who's sitting at a desk near the back.

"Well, we'd better catch up with the rest of *our* family," Dad says. "Good to see you, Rip."

"You too!" He's still chortling as we walk out of adult baking.

"What's so funny about being a baking judge?" I ask once we're outside.

Now Dad laughs. "I'll bet Rip Hansen sometimes *wishes* he was a baking judge," he says. "He's the superintendent of the *whole Fair*. He works on the Fair year-round, and he's working every minute the Fair is open. He has to be everywhere at once, and they call for him on the loudspeakers all day long." Dad curls his hand in front of his mouth and toots like a trumpet. "Rip's responsible for everything and everyone here. Which reminds me," Dad adds, "the next time you see him you should tell him your name is Miller, not Merwin."

"Oh, he knows." I reach back and check the huge rip in my T-shirt again. "He knows."

30
THE UNIVERSE OF FAIR

"Sorry about your ribbon, Miller," Mrs. Noyes says when we come into the youth exhibit.

"That's okay," I tell her. "Maybe I'll get a ribbon next year."

"You'll get your ribbon *this* year!" She smiles. "I don't know how it got knocked down, but it's back up there now. Go take a look!"

Penny and Mom are standing in front of my "physics collection" when Dad and I get there.

"I'm going to be a baking judge next year," I tell Mom.

"You got a red!" Penny yells.

"Congratulations!" Mom says. "On both things!"

She hugs me and Penny hugs me and Dad hugs all of us. Big night for hugs.

Mrs. Noyes comes over and pulls me aside. "I shouldn't tell you this," she looks over her shoulder and lowers her voice. "The judges said your ribbon would have been a blue except this isn't really a collection. And those judges are—"

"Sticklers for rules," I say. "I know."

"But they loved your project, Miller. *Loved* it! So they're adding a new category to the youth exhibit, starting next year. Hands-on Science!"

Mrs. Noyes, the nicest grown-up in the world, goes back to her seat at the front of the building.

I grin. Hands-on Science. I can do that.

We wave good-bye to Mrs. Noyes and walk out of the youth exhibit. Dad holds tight to Penny's hand.

"Miller," Mom says. "Penny's been telling me all about everything that's happened today." She gives me a knowing look.

I stop smiling. I stop walking. "*Everything?*" I ask.

"Oh yes. Everything," she says, looking slightly dazed. "And even though it's apparently been an eventful day, here we are together, with everyone fine and accounted for."

I think for a minute. "Even at your work?"

"Yes, honey, even at my work. Our friend went to visit her cousin all the way up in New Roxborough without telling anyone. But she's back where she's supposed to be," Mom says with a relieved smile. "So I was thinking about all of the responsibilities you took on today, and about how careful you tried to be in spite of how hard it was."

"It was so hard, Mom," I say.

"I know today was nothing like the Fair day you expected, but how about some Fair time on your own right now? All things considered, I think you've earned it. Let's say…ten minutes?"

"A whole ten minutes?" Dad teases.

Mom takes a deep breath. "Okay…fifteen. You can meet us on the concert hill. We'll pick up dinner on the way."

Dad puts his arm around Mom. "This is very brave of you, Dana," he says.

"I *will* worry," she says. "But I'll try not to overdo it."

I look around at the fairgrounds spreading out in front of us: beautiful, noisy, and crammed full of people. I'm reasonably sure I've had enough responsible and careful to last me until next year—or maybe even the year after. Lewis is gone and I'm starving, so sitting on the hill with my parents and eating a Fair dinner is all I really want to do. But then I remember something important.

"Go ahead, then," Mom says.

"Okay," I say.

"Meet us at the concert," she says. "On the side of the hill where we always sit."

"In fifteen minutes," I say.

"We'll be next to the telephone pole. The third pole," she adds.

"I know."

"Counting from the stage."

"See you there," Dad says, steering Mom and Penny down the path.

I look around at the food booths and the exhibits. Music from the concert floats across the Fair. Down the hill, people are moving in and out of the animal barns. The Ferris Wheel is turning at the edge of the midway, the BlastoCoaster is zooming, and the Gravity Whirl is up at the top of its spin. In a strange way, the Fair feels bigger *and* smaller to me than it ever has, and I can feel its powerful force field all around. Fifteen minutes isn't a lot of time. I hope it will be enough.

Even though I've run about six marathons already today, I race up the hill one last time. I run all the way up to the town green and join the eighty-seven thousand people browsing in the crafts tent.

I dodge and weave through the aisles, passing doll sweaters, pottery, jars of jam, and dog leashes. The dog leash place has a bowl of free biscuits, so I pocket one for the Wonderdog. I keep going past fleece hats, hand-painted bird houses, and wooden animals. None of those things are what I want.

But then I see just the right kind of stall. I examine every item closely until I find the exact, perfect thing.

"How much for this pink, purple, and yellow heart-shaped pin?" I ask the jewelry seller.

"That one?" she points. "Eighteen dollars."

I pull the rest of my Fair savings out of my pocket. I count it, as if the three-fifty I had left after the games plus the ten dollars Andrew's mother gave me could magically add up to eighteen. It doesn't.

"Thanks, anyway," I say. I turn away.

"Wait. How much you got?" the jewelry seller asks.

"Only thirteen-fifty," I tell her.

"Sold!" She hands me the pin, tucked in a fancy velvet jewelry box.

"Thanks!" I say. "Thanks a lot!"

I pay and dash out of the crafts tent. Now I can't wait for Tuesday. Mom is going to love her birthday present. I race over to the concert hill and find my family with half a minute to spare.

"MOM BOUGHT YOU A HOLMSBURY FAIR T-SHIRT AND A HOLMSBURY FAIR BASEBALL CAP," my sister yells so everyone on the next planet can hear her.

"I want a T-shirt, too," someone calls out.

"Penny, you told," Mom laughs. "I was going to wrap them and give them to you in the morning."

"Thanks, Mom," I say. "That's the best present ever!" Almost, I think, patting the box in my pocket.

"You earned them," Mom says.

"And this is for you, too." Dad hands me a ten-dollar bill.

"But I already got my ten dollars back for Lou-Ann's ride bracelet," I tell him. "Andrew's mother gave it to me."

"That ten dollars is for tomorrow," Dad says, "so you and Lewis can go on the Gravity Whirl and whatever else you can fit in before you watch the judges do the state bake-off."

"The Gravity Whirl?" I say, not quite understanding.

Mom smiles weakly. "We've been talking about this, and I decided that since you have to come anyway, and I missed today, I'm going to bring you at ten and sub for someone at the lemonade cart. Do you think you can figure out what to do with yourselves for a couple of hours?"

"You mean like rides and stuff? On my own with Lewis?" I gulp. "You're not kidding?"

"Not kidding," Dad says.

Now I do jump up and down. "Wow," I shout. "Thanks! I can't believe this!" I leap in the air again, then flop down so tired that I wonder, just for a moment, if I've dreamed this or what. I can't wait to call Lewis.

"I get to come to the Fair on Saturday as soon as I'm eleven and a half, too," my sister says.

Mom passes me a bowl of Garden Club chili and a tall chocolate milkshake. I take one fiery spoonful of chili at a time and cool it off with a swig of shake.

Dad starts singing along with the band. "You gotta rock, in this world, you gotta rock."

Penny dumps the midway prizes out onto the blanket. She puts all of the spider rings we won on her fingers and makes them talk to the big green dog, the purple giraffe, and the three goldfish.

When I finish eating, I stretch out on the blanket so I can see the stars winking overhead—trillions and trillions

of them—so many that if I stare long enough it feels like I'm falling up into them. I wonder why all of the subatomic, string-theory strings that make up me, Miller Sanford, are vibrating here on Earth instead of on some other planet, or even in some other galaxy. Then I think about how there could be a kid in some other galaxy looking up into his sky and wondering about *his* subatomic strings. Maybe his galaxy is in one of those extra dimensions, or in a parallel universe where he's just lived through the longest, hardest, worryingest day in his entire life and almost lost his six-year-old sister, too.

"Hey, Penny," I say. I push myself up onto my elbow. "On our way out, want to go back through the youth exhibit and show me which part of the pear butter is yours?"

"That's dumb," one of Pain-elope's spider fingers tells the giraffe. "Pear butter doesn't have parts."

"Right," I say. "No parts." And I go back to watching the stars.

ACKNOWLEDGMENTS

I would like to thank the many people who contributed immeasurably to the creation of this book, including Doe Boyle, Judy Theise, Kay Kudlinski, Leslie Connor, Lorraine Jay, Mary-Kelly Busch, Nancy Antle, Nancy Elizabeth Wallace, Peter Banks, Joel Wachman, L. Blair Hewes, Vicky Holifield, E. Brooks Holifield, Amy Brittain, Loraine Joyner, Mabel Hamma, Madison Holdmeyer, Dormer Labs, Peachtree Publishers, and all of my Fair friends who shared their stories with me, and who make the Fair wonderful every year.

The two poetic gravestone inscriptions used in the story are altered versions of existing Connecticut epitaphs. Bits of Durham, Connecticut, history were snipped, clipped, and jumbled in my mental tumbler to create Holmsbury's fictional ghost story.

All characters in this story are entirely fictional and bear no resemblance to real people, with the exception of Mrs. Noyes, about whom Miller is entirely correct: she's the nicest grown-up in the world.

Leslie Bulion has graduate degrees in oceanography and social work. She has written parenting and education articles and is the author of several children's books, including UNCHARTED WATERS, THE TROUBLE WITH RULES, and AT THE SEA FLOOR CAFÉ. Leslie lives in Connecticut with her husband, Rubin Hirsch, and at the youth exhibit of her town's agricultural fair, come fall.
www.lesliebulion.com

Frank W. Dormer, a graduate of the Savannah College of Art and Design, is an elementary school art teacher. In addition to illustrating many children's books, he wrote and illustrated THE OBSTINATE PEN and SOCKSQUATCH. He has drawn dogs, kids, cowboys, pens, imaginary creatures, and now thanks to Leslie Bulion, bumper cars. Frank lives in Branford, Connecticut.
www.frankwdormer.com